OPERATION: NORTH POLE

WILLIAM MEIKLE

SEVEREDPRESS

OPERATION: NORTH POLE

- MARGARET -

Just that very morning Margaret Paterson had been wishing for some excitement.

A research expedition to the North Pole should, in her mind, be a thing of adventure and pioneering spirit. But if truth be told she might as well have been back in the lab in Milton Keynes.

Purpose-built laboratories and living quarters had been made especially for the expedition, state of the art technology, its standards informed by research out of a collaboration between NASA and the British Antarctic Survey. Maximum effort had been spent to ensure the scientific team would be as comfortable as possible. They were thoroughly insulated against anything the weather could throw at them, so much so that she often felt like an experiment herself, sealed in the three hermetic domes that enclosed the whole of her world for the duration.

She didn't even get to collect samples out on the ice; her days were bound by tedium, the only exercise she got was walking between the gas spectrometer and her terminal, and their nights were spent in an endless round of card games or bland movies. There wasn't even a view to look at out of the window, for although spring was coming, it wasn't here yet and they were still in the darkness of the Arctic winter. Boredom had set in weeks ago, and there were still more long weeks of it stretching out ahead of her.

As it turned out, she should have been careful what she wished for.

When it happened, it happened fast. She'd headed for the refectory dead on the stroke of twelve noon, hoping to beat the queue, but half a dozen others had the same idea and were in line waiting for the hatch to open to the kitchen.

Today's menu was a choice of spag bol or fried chicken. She'd had more than enough of both in the previous weeks for neither of them to hold much enthusiasm for her, but she needed the fuel.

She was debating with herself which was the most palatable of the options when there was the crack of a gunshot outside, then an almighty crash, also from somewhere outside, followed quickly by the distant sound of screams, mingled with more gunfire, far too much gunfire. A cold blast of air ran through the dome.

Somebody just opened a door. Bad idea.

Many of the people in the refectory ran towards the source of the sound, heading for the doors that led towards Dome Three.

That was the same area that was the source of the cold air. Margaret credited herself with more smarts than that. She headed in the opposite direction from the fracas, making for the door to the corridor that led to her lab area in Dome One. The distant but clearly recognisable sound of more gunfire came from behind her as she turned away.

She broke into a trot, almost jogging. Suddenly she felt the need to be somewhere, anywhere but here.

She knew that distance might not mean safety.

But it's a damn sight safer than running towards screaming and gunfire.

She was halfway across the canteen when there was another loud crash behind her; she didn't waste time looking back, but now the screaming was closer, coming from people in the same room as her. The cold breeze went up a notch, a strong wind now pushing at her back, urging her forward. She put on a burst of speed.

She wasn't the only one trying to leave. The doorway ahead was crowded with too many people all attempting to get through it at the same time. It was a free-for-all, one in which Margaret was more than happy to join in, despite pleas and exhortations from a voice shouting for calm. She threw herself into the melee, pulled a man a good foot taller than her aside and jumped into the vacated space. She saw the corridor that led to Dome One ahead of her, saw the open door leading into the lab beyond. She also saw that the people in there were trying to close that door, despite the fact there were still more than a dozen people making for it.

"Oh no you don't," she screamed, put her head down and ran full pelt. The cold air rushing in behind her was ravenous; she felt it bite at the back of her neck and at her ankles.

She got halfway along the corridor before there was another crash behind her, another loud, bestial roar.

The lights failed and the screams sounded like they were coming from just behind her, right at her heels.

She didn't slow, couldn't afford to.

She ran in darkness.

- WIGGO -

Wiggo had several things on his mind, the least of which was the fact they were only ten minutes out from jumping out of a plane, in the dark, over the North Pole. The main thing worrying him was young Davies. The corporal wasn't himself and hadn't been for a while now. Wiggo had been putting it down to losing the new lads in Patagonia and had been cutting the man some slack.

It looks like I've cut him too much.

Davies sat apart from the others at the rear of the plane, gazing at something only he could see in the distance.

"He's your pal," Wiggo said to Wilkins in the seat beside him. Wiggo had sat down just minutes before, and the discussion had turned to Davies' recent erratic behavior.

"His report on the Orkney thing was a mess. The Colonel had words with the Captain about it, I ken that much. The Captain's still covering Davies' arse… for now," Wiggo said. "And that's not breaking any confidentiality. You and I ken the lad well enough to ken he's no' got his head screwed on right these days."

Wilkins looked glum and only nodded in reply.

"What's up with him... and don't give me any shite about Patagonia. I'm no' daft. I ken it's something else," Wiggo pressed.

"I've tried talking to him, Sarge. Even offered to stand for a pint and a curry if he had something to get off his chest. But it was no deal. It's like talking to a brick wall."

"It's no' talking to it I'm thinking about. I'm thinking about banging his heid against it."

Wiggo had intended to have a word that very morning, but the briefing had been called at short notice, then they'd moved out double time to get kitted up, and there had been no opportunity to get the lad aside for a confab. Davies wasn't about to volunteer anything without prompting; he hadn't said a word since that briefing, which had been short and sweet. The Colonel had summarized it in a couple of sentences.

"There's a British research team at the North Pole gone quiet all of a sudden. We need you up there sharpish to see what's what."

Once kitted up in Arctic gear and in the air the Captain had shared an email detailing the facility they were headed for; Wiggo had only paid it a cursory glance.

It's a group of fugly buildings. It's dark. And it's fucking cold. What else do I need to know?

There was one other thing niggling at Wiggo. Apart from the imminent drop and the state of Davies' mental health, they were also men short on the op; they'd been promised two new team members. Wiggo had hand-picked them from the available roster, but they hadn't had their assignments yet and the Colonel wasn't pushing too hard for 'budgetary reasons'.

If we have to carry Davies as dead weight and we end up too short staffed for the op, the Colonel will find out exactly where he can stuff his budget.

The overhead green light turned red and the back hangar door of the plane opened. Then there was no time for any kind of talk at all.

Wiggo went out first, immediately after the chute that took down their gear. He followed the orange flare down; it wasn't quite full-dark below him, more like the time between sunset and night, and he was able to make out the triple-domed shape of the facility below his feet. Even from a height he saw that one of the domes was crushed in across one side, gaping like a broken egg shell.

They've had some trouble.

He looked up to check that the others were following him down then concentrated on keeping his trajectory in line with the flare below. The lower he dropped, the colder it got. He felt the cold nip at the tip of his nose, just about the only part of him exposed to it, and felt icy wind tug at his legs, bitter even through the insulated layers of their winter survival gear.

Should have gone to Benidorm.

He landed, harder than he would have liked, on ice that felt like rock, and his chute, caught by a breeze, threatened to topple him over backward before he got it under control. By the time he was winding the material in the Captain was down by his side. Wilkins hit the ground hard next, and let off a whelp of pain; Wiggo guessed the lad's bad legs were still bothering him, but nobody mentioned it. Davies landed last, and stood away silently to one side as he rolled up his own chute.

The silence of the night was broken by a loud honking klaxon from one of the two surviving domes, three sharp blasts that weren't repeated before the quiet fell over them again. Cold bit hard at them as they made their way to the chute that had brought down their kit.

"Saddle up, lads," Banks said. "The sooner we get under shelter the better I'll feel."

They retrieved their rifles and helmets from the kit bags, stowed all the chutes into a single bag and left it anchored on the ice in case they needed to retrieve them later, eased themself into their rucksacks and were soon lined up facing the domes. The farthest left dome was the shattered one, and the one farthest right had lights showing in the windows. Banks pointed right.

"Let's see if there's a welcome party waiting for us. Look sharp, lads, and game faces on. We don't know what we're walking into."

Banks led them out. Wiggo let the two younger men pass him and took up the rear. He scanned the horizon. The sky was slightly lighter way to the east, but only marginally so, and there was nothing to see but a plain of snow and ice in every direction. By the time he turned round the others were already making for the lights of the third dome and he had to put on a spurt of speed to catch up. The ground underfoot was treacherously slippery, but his stout boots held their grip and he fell into the long practiced loping stride that allowed him to travel for long distances carrying a heavy pack. Thankfully they didn't have far to go.

As they approached the dome they heard the distinctive creak of metal on metal. A door opened revealing a figure in shadow, backlit by bright lights inside. A woman shouted.

"For fuck's sake hurry up and get inside. It's not safe out there."

Wiggo held back, watching out onto the ice while the others hurried inside. He didn't step back until he was sure the coast was clear, even when the woman shouted again in his ear.

"Are you fucking deaf or something. Get in here. It's not safe."

"Keep your knickers on," he said. "I heard you the first time. I was just ignoring you."

She was still searching for a comeback when he stepped past her into the dome. The door was swung shut at their back, the clang echoing around them. They were in a corridor that ran around the perimeter of the dome. Apart from the woman who had ushered them in, three other people stood looking at the newly arrived soldiers; a woman and two men, all swaddled in clothes, so much so that they looked almost comically bear-like.

"Are you supposed to be the cavalry?" the woman who had shown them inside said, the sarcasm clear in her voice.

"Aye," Wiggo answered. "We're looking for a damsel in distress. You haven't seen one hanging about, have you?"

"Aren't you a bit short for a stormtrooper?"

"Oh, so it's like that, is it?" Wiggo replied, smiling. He didn't get a smile in reply and before he could continue Banks' voice cut in.

"Who's in charge here?" he said.

One of the men stepped forward.

"I guess that's me," he said. He peeled off a fur-lined glove and put out a hand for Banks to shake. "George Collins, senior geologist. Nominally, Ed Baxter is in charge, but he was in Dome Three and..."

Banks stopped him.

"Back up. I'll need the story of what's happened here, and I need it soon, but I'll need it all, and I'll need it in the right order. Any chance of a coffee?"

"A man after my own heart," Collins said. "Right this way; it's about the only thing we can still rely on."

Collins led Banks and the others along the corridor and through a door into the interior of the dome. Wiggo was about to follow when he noticed that Davies had hung back and was standing with his back to the others. Wiggo stepped over, caught him by the shoulder and turned him around, just in time to see the younger man try to hurriedly put something into his inside pocket. Wiggo snatched it out of his hand and studied it; it was a small medical ampule, blue glass, broken open at one end. Wiggo sniffed at it; it smelled heady and Wiggo had been hospitalized enough times to make a good guess at what had been inside.

"Morphine? You're taking fucking morphine on an op?"

"Let it go, Sarge. It's nothing to concern you. It's just a wee pick-me-up of my own devising. I'm under control, honest; it's just to take the edge off."

"I'll take your fucking edge off for you, son," Wiggo said. "Fucking pick-me-up? Is that what they're calling this shite these days? Well here's something that'll pick you up. When we get back to the world, you're going to take a blood test. You and I both ken that you'll fail it, and that'll be the end of it. And one more thing. As of right now, you're busted; Wilkins is acting corporal, and you're somewhere lower than a private; in fact, consider yourself at about the level of shite I'd scrape off my shoe."

"You cannae dae that, Sarge."

"Can I no'? Just fucking watch me. Fucking morphine? I had you down for mair sense. Mair fool me."

"I can explain…"

"Naw. Ye cannae. No' tae me right now at any case, for I'm no' listening. Save it for the disciplinary hearing…if you even get that far. My guess is you'll be oot on your arse ten minutes after we get back to Lossiemouth; the Captain takes an even dimmer view than I do of this sort of buggeration. Now fuck off and get a coffee before I'm tempted to open that door and kick you back outside."

Davies turned away, then Wiggo called him back.

"Before you go, you'd better give me any more of that shite you've got hidden on you."

He saw the rebellion rise in Davies' stare, but Wiggo wasn't about to back down, not on this. For four, maybe five seconds he thought Davies might hit him. Then the younger man's gaze dropped, his shoulders slumped and he reached into his jacket to bring out five more blue glass ampules, all still whole.

"That's the lot? You're sure?"

"I wouldnae lie to you, Sarge," Davies said.

"No? It's all you've been doing recently. How the fuck am I supposed to believe a word that comes out of your mouth? Fuck off; I don't want to be looking at you for a while."

Davies left to follow the others.

Wiggo held back just long enough to drop the ampules to the floor and stomp them down under his boot until all that was left was a wet smear and a blue patch of finely ground glass.

- WILKINS -

Wilkins saw Davies come into the dome; the corporal looked like a whipped dog, and when Wiggo entered at his back he saw that the Sarge had a face like thunder. But whatever had happened, it didn't look like there was going to be an immediate explanation, for the man, Collins, was already leading them through what was obviously a working laboratory, even if all the electrical gear looked to have been shut down. The room was warmer than the outside, but you wouldn't exactly call it toasty. There was ice on the inside of the windows, and the condensation of their breath steamed as they spoke.

"Sorry we can't be more hospitable. We've been conserving energy," Collins said. "We've mostly been living in here."

He brought them to a central area where chairs and tables had been moved aside and a makeshift tent had been built from storage containers, upturned tables, sheets and carpets. They all made their way inside, having to crouch to gain entry. The inner space was decidedly warmer and was dominated by four heavy duty sleeping bags on camp cots, and a small propane stove. With all eight of them inside they were going to be very cramped for space.

"This is going to be cozy," Wiggo said.

"Not for long," the woman who'd let them in replied, but didn't elaborate.

Collins wheeled the stove into the tent's entrance and began boiling up a kettle of water while everyone else tried to find a place to crouch or sit. Wiggo went back outside the makeshift tent into the lab area and they heard the distinctive sound of his Zippo lighter clack and clatter as he lit up a smoke.

"He shouldn't be doing that," Collins said. "It's not safe."

"Trust me," Banks said, "it's not safe to try to stop him."

Banks waited until Collins got the kettle going before he spoke again.

"Okay, give me the bad news. What's happened here?"

Collins was quiet for several seconds, gathering his thoughts before he spoke, and when he did it was in a dull monotone, as if relating events that had happened somewhere else, to somebody else.

"We arrived on site at the back end of last summer. We even caught a bit of good weather for the first couple of weeks. Ed Baxter had been here for a few months before that, supervising construction, and it had all gone as smoothly as these things ever do. As I say, the scientific team, myself included, arrived later, but we got settled in just fine.

"We got through the winter with only minor problems," he continued. "The new domes stood up to the conditions admirably, our experiments were all proceeding as planned and we were collecting good data on ocean currents and ice sheet movements in particular. We even managed to keep warm, mostly, although I couldn't say we were ever exactly cozy.

"It all changed just over forty-eight hours ago. We'd had attention from polar bears several times earlier in the winter, but Rory Brown, our security guy, was always able to scare them off by firing a shot over their heads from his hunting rifle. We stopped paying too much attention to them; once they realized there was no food to be had from us, they mostly left us alone.

"Then, as I said, everything changed. I was in the lab here working through lunch. We'd had a new batch of ice core samples brought in and I wanted to get them stored away before I took a break. That probably saved my life.

"When I heard a gunshot, I assumed it was another polar bear incident and that Rory had the matter well in hand. Then the screaming started, coming from the direction of the central dome, where we have…had… the living quarters and refectory. There were more gunshots.

"I rushed along the corridor to Dome Two to see what was going on. There was chaos. Most people were by the window overlooking Dome Three, although some were beginning to head in my direction. I had a clear view out of the big window opposite, although in the gloom it took a while to make out what

I was seeing, and even longer still to believe it. A great white beast was rampaging among the wreckage of the dome, throwing the contents hither and thither across the ice… and some of those contents were people, friends of mine. I saw it trample poor Rory, face down, into the cold ground, saw his body come apart under the pressure. I had to turn away at that, but I couldn't block out the sounds of the screams.

"Somebody shouted, 'It's coming this way'.

"That's when the panic started. Some of us made it to the door to get in here. Others tried another exit. The lights went out about that point, although I can't rightly be sure I've got everything straight in my head, for there was a lot of panic. The four of us got in here eventually and slammed the door behind us. The backup generator kicked in, which is what's keeping us alive right now, and I finally found and hit the emergency klaxon; it's been going off intermittently ever since. We think the noise keeps the bear away…at least it hasn't come back."

"Yet," the woman said, earning her a black look from Collins.

"And the other people?" Banks asked softly.

Collins went pale and shook his head.

"We just don't know. We heard screams. Then silence."

"You didn't go to look?"

The man went paler still, and just shook his head again.

"What about comms?" Banks asked.

"Outside communication was via a dish above Dome Three. The main generator was under it. We're guessing the bear took out both the comms and the power," the woman who had let them in said. "We've had nothing in or out since it was destroyed."

Banks took out his satphone, preparing to dial.

"It won't work," the woman said. "We've got one just like it; we get nothing but static."

Banks tried anyway, a puzzled look crossing his face when he couldn't get a dialing tone. He turned back to Collins.

"You're telling me a single polar bear took out a state of the art facility and massacred most of the staff, including your armed man?" he said.

"No," Collins said, scarcely above a whisper. "You weren't listening. I'm telling you it wasn't a polar bear, at least, not just a polar bear."

"What do you mean by that?"

The woman responded.

"It was fucking massive, that's what he means by that; the fucker was as big as a house, and angry with it. It tore through the dome walls as if it was balsa wood."

The kettle came to the boil and whistled. At the same moment the single overhead bulb that lit the interior of the makeshift tent flickered, threatened to go out, then came back strong again.

"Another one bites the dust," the woman said bitterly, then explained. "It does that when the generator has to move onto another diesel tank. By my reckoning we've got two tanks left."

"How long?" Banks asked.

"Twenty-four hours, max," Collins replied. "Then it goes totally dark and we really start to freeze."

"Do you have any more fuel?"

"Maybe under Dome Three, where the original generator was housed. But that might have gone along with the comms and power. But checking on that means going outside. The bear's outside."

It looked like Collins was done talking; the man busied himself getting a pot of coffee on the go. Banks addressed the woman; she was the only one of the four survivors who didn't look to be almost catatonic with shock.

"How many are missing?" he asked.

"We were thirty, now we're four. Simple maths."

"Is there a chance some of them might be hiding in Dome Two? Trying to wait it out like you've been doing here?"

"As far as I know there's no light or heat in there," she said. "After forty-eight hours, they'll be icicles."

"No backup generator?"

"No, the one here was to keep the lab machines running if the main one failed. The living quarters didn't have one. I'm telling you, they're all dead."

"We have to go look," Banks said. "It's why we're here."

She waved a hand towards the exit to the tented structure.

"Don't let it hit your arse on the way out," she said.

Wiggo came in, summonsed by the smell of coffee.

"I need a word with you, Cap," Wiggo said.

"I'm listening," Banks replied.

"No, in private, and official like. Let's take our coffee out into the lab. This can't wait."

Wilkins was the only one to note the pointed look that passed between Wiggo and the sullenly silent Davies.

What the fuck is going on here?

He thought about asking Davies, but one look at the corporal's face was enough to tell him that wasn't an option.

He took his coffee outside, hoping to mooch a smoke from the Sarge and maybe find out what was going down, but the conversation was already over. Wiggo looked to be in a foul mood. So did the Captain for that matter, and when Banks turned his attention to Wilkins, the younger man began wondering what it was he had done wrong. The Captain sensed his nervousness.

"No, it's not you, lad, you can rest easy on that. But I need a word with you. We've talked before about how you would have been next up for corporal before your injury in London. Well, it's here, now. As of right now, you're acting corporal, and we'll make it official when we get back to base."

"But Davies…"

"No buts, lad. Just take it for what it is. You're now Corporal Wilkins, and he's busted back to Private Davies. If he gives you a problem about it, deal with it as you see fit, or come to me or the Sarge. Either way, the deal is done."

"What did he do?"

"You'll find out soon enough."

Davies had screwed up somehow, that much was obvious, but it was equally obvious that the conversation with the captain was now over; Banks was once again in confab with the Sarge, both of them keeping their voices low.

Wilkins went back into the makeshift tent. Davies looked up.

"Happy now?" the former corporal said.

"Far from it," Wilkins replied. "How about you? Want to talk about it?"

He didn't get a reply; Davies turned his head away and fell back into a sullen silence.

- MARGARET -

She didn't think much of the cavalry. Then again, she didn't think much of herself. She'd been trying unsuccessfully to blot out the memory of that flight along the corridor in the dark. She remembered trampling, not on hard floor, but on soft bodies, remembered the shrieks and squeals of pain. None of it had stopped her; she'd run full pelt, her arms stretched out ahead of her as if grasping for the door.

Somebody grabbed her by the left wrist, and it was her turn to scream, until a voice spoke in her ear and a flashlight was waved, too bright, in her face.

"I've got you."

It was Collins, a voice of stability and sanity amid the chaos. She held onto it like a drowning woman to a lifebelt and let him drag her forwards, out of the corridor and into the lab. Dim lights were just coming on as the generator kicked in. Apart from her and Collins there were only two other people present, hugging the far wall as if ready to flee even farther should it be necessary.

She turned in time to see Collins close the corridor door and stand with his back to it. There were still faint sounds of screaming on the other side.

"We've got to let them in," she said.

"Do we really?" Collins said. He spoke calmly, but the terror showed clearly in his eyes. And before she could reply the sounds of screams had died away on the other side of the doorway, leaving them in deathly silence.

After that it had become a matter of survival; making the makeshift tent, locating what supplies they could muster, and trying in vain to get out a distress call, all the while trying not to think of what had happened on the far side of the doors.

"You didn't tell them everything," she said accusingly to Collins. "You didn't tell them we were bloody cowards."

"No. And you didn't tell them either. What's your point?"

She didn't have one. All she had was her guilt, and the memory of the screams behind the locked doors.

Now the cavalry was here. They'd be going through those same doors.

Margaret's shame was about to be uncovered, and she wasn't happy at the prospect.

- WIGGO -

"If it was possible, I'd leave you back there with the civvies for the duration," Banks said. The four of them were standing by the door that would open into Dome Two. Davies had his head down, unable to look the Captain in the eye. "But it's not possible. I need the extra gun. So, are you going to at least try to be a good soldier? Do I have your word?"

Davies merely nodded, but Wiggo knew that was enough for the Cap, for now at least. Davies hadn't looked any of them in the eye since his secret came out, but beneath the sullen glares he was still a soldier, still a squad member, and Wiggo could only hope the lad might remember that before his woes took him too far on a downward spiral. All they could do for now was trust his sense of duty.

If there's any left in him.

Banks took the lead again and opened the door that led to the corridor beyond. It was pitch black dark ahead and an icy blast of air washed over them. Without needing an order they all pulled up their parka hoods, zipping them up over their chins, and pulled down their goggles so that only the tips of their noses showed. Even then the cold was biting.

"Let's get this done quick," Banks said, and stepped forward.

"It's not looking promising," Wiggo said.

"Let's get a sweep done anyway," Banks replied. "Maybe they've got a wee tent like the first lot."

They closed the door behind them as they went through into the short corridor that led between the domes. The beams of the lights on their rifles drew ovals on walls that were coated in a liberal layer of hoar frost and their footsteps crunched on the crispy surface on the floor. There was no sign of any footprints.

The corridor led into another, the second dome, what the survivors said was the refectory area. It was empty save for a few tumbled tables and chairs. The first three doors off from this room led into dormitory rooms each containing ranks of bunk beds along the walls. The beds were all empty, although the bedding was still in place; Wiggo realized this was bad news for any theory of a makeshift shelter having been built, but kept his mouth shut. This place felt less of a dwelling, more of a tomb, and an air of grim fatality had settled on the squad members as they went back into the corridor.

They went back into the main interior of the dome, the mess hall and kitchen area. They checked the space thoroughly. There was no sign of life.

"Where the fuck did they go?" Wiggo whispered.

They found the answer on the far side of the dome. An exterior door was open, the source of the cold. A pile of bodies...what was left of them... filled the doorway and spilled out onto the ice outside.

"Christ on a bike, they look like they've gone through a woodchipper," Wiggo said.

The snow was spattered, Jackson-Pollock red on white in a wide fan beyond the doorway, the iced blood punctuated with gobbets of flesh, fragments of clothing, and the gleam of too-white broken bones. A narrow trail of blood led away towards the ruin of the third dome, as if one or more bodies had been dragged in that direction.

Banks didn't hesitate; he stepped gingerly over the bodies in the doorway and made his way out into the dark. At first Wiggo thought that Davies was going to refuse to go, but once Wilkins went after the Captain, the newly-demoted private followed at his back. Wiggo guessed shame was proving to be a motivator, but he kept a close eye on Davies as they brought up the rear and they made their way slowly towards the crumpled ruin of Dome Three.

The west-facing wall of the dome looked like it had been hit by a bus, one that had impacted at speed and kept going until it was well inside. The wall was bent inward in places and the shattered remains showed where a large window had once stood. The blood trail stopped at the hole in the wall, and the interior was shrouded in dark shadows. Some of the floor area had collapsed down into a basement. If there had been a generator down there it was now under several feet of ice and snow and well beyond repair.

Wiggo sniffed at the air but could smell nothing. All he felt was the chill as the small hairs in his nostrils immediately froze. He pulled his mouth and nose down inside the top fur-lined edge of his parka and kept it there until feeling returned.

They all stood looking into the darkness of the crushed dome. If there was a beast in there, it was probably looking back, but, to Wiggo's gut anyway, the place felt empty and abandoned. The Captain wasn't about to take any chances though.

"Slow and steady, lads," Banks said over the radio. He motioned Wilkins forward to his side. "Two by two," he said. "And canny."

Davies still wouldn't look Wiggo in the eye as they moved shoulder to shoulder behind the others and they stepped into the dome.

It was colder still here, biting through their clothing, like a sudden immersion in cold water. More body parts lay strewn across the floor of what was obviously another laboratory area, but again the place felt as dead and cold as a tomb. His gut had proved right; if there had been a beastie here, it was long gone.

They did a sweep of the whole area to be sure, but all they found was more blood and gore. A partial trail of bloody footprints, roughly oval-shaped and each of them more than two feet long, led out of the dome and off to the northwest into the gloom. Wiggo lifted his rifle and aimed the light beam in that direction.

Something wailed, half-bark, half-scream in the distance then everything went quiet again. They stood listening. There was no more sound out in the night. The klaxon went off in Dome One breaking the silence and Wiggo twitched, startled. At the same instant Davies raised his gun and sent three wild shots out into the gloom.

"For fuck's sake, lad," Banks said. "When I said slow and steady, I meant it. Do that again and I'll take it off you. Understand?"

Before Davies could reply another roar came from the northwest, louder than the last.

"I think we got its attention. It's coming closer," Wiggo said.

"Take cover," Banks ordered. "Wiggo, Davies, go left, we'll go right, see if we can catch it in crossfire. And Davies…if you fuck this up, it'll be the last thing you ever do on this squad."

Wiggo hurried Davies to the left, found a hefty table and turned it over so they could shelter behind it, although if this fucker was as big as its footprints indicated, a table wasn't going to be much protection at all.

A third roar echoed across the ice, much closer now.

"Wait for it," Banks said in Wiggo's earpiece. They heard its approach, a thunder of feet beating on ice. Wiggo looked over the top of the table and saw it coming; it looked like a train approaching them, a white, bear-shaped train, all mouth and teeth and bellowing rage. He estimated its height at eight feet at the shoulder, and it looked like it was made mostly of muscle.

"Wait for it," Banks said again.

It was close now, no more than twenty yards away; even if they took it down, its momentum was going to have it barrelling into them.

"Fire!" Banks shouted, and the air was suddenly full of the crack of their rifles. The bear bellowed, a howl of pain, and veered off sharply to the west, taking cover behind the remaining dome wall, lost from their sight. Everything fell quiet save for the ringing in Wiggo's ears from the gunfire.

"Did we get it?" Davies said at his side.

"I certainly hit something," Wiggo replied. "But it's a damned big bugger. Looks like we didnae slow it down much."

Banks and Wilkins stood up from behind their table.

"Anybody see it?" Banks asked over the radio.

"All clear this side, as far as I can tell," Wiggo replied.

Banks motioned that Wiggo should cover him as he stepped forward into the open area at the crushed part of the dome. He looked east and west across the ice, then motioned the others forward.

"Looks like it's buggered off for now," he said. "Come on, let's get back and get some coffee inside us. We need a cunning plan."

Wiggo hung back and studied the snow where the trail went northwest; there were fresh footprints there now, and new splashes of blood.

"There's fresh blood spatter here," he said over the radio. "We've given it something to yell about, at least."

"Let's hope yelling is all it decides to do, for now," Banks replied, then Wiggo had to hurry to catch the others up on the way back to the lights in Dome Three.

- WILKINS -

Coffee and a smoke back in Dome One proved most welcome after their trip over the ice. The Captain was in the makeshift tent with the survivors, briefing them on their findings. Wilkins didn't envy him the prospect; it was a bleak message to have to deliver. He stood with Wiggo near the tent's entrance; Davies was sitting on a chair off to one side, head down, incommunicative.

"What the fuck did he do, Sarge?" Wilkins asked, keeping his voice low so only the two of them could hear.

"He let himself down. He let the squad down," Wiggo said. The Sarge didn't bother lowering his voice, and Wilkins saw Davies' head drop lower as the words sunk in.

"How bad is it?"

"Bad enough. My guess is he'll be getting his jotters as soon as we get back. The Captain won't have a druggie on the squad."

Wilkins was about to say that the Sarge must be mistaken, then remembered their most recent op, in Orkney, and Davies offering him 'a wee pick-me-up'.

Oh, pal. What have you gone and done?

His first instinct was to go to his friend. His second was to stay well away, give Davies time to process the fact that his life had just changed irretrievably. He stayed where he was at the tent opening and Davies stayed, head down, in the chair, only five yards away but it felt like the other side of the planet.

A possibly awkward silence was broken when Banks came back out of the tent. He addressed Wiggo and Wilkins, not even giving Davies so much as a glance.

"Well, they took that about as well as could be expected. I'd leave them alone for a bit. They've got a lot to process."

He lit up a smoke before continuing.

"I might have a plan. But I doubt you'll like it. As I see it we've got two problems; one is the bear... we've all already seen the size of that problem... and the other is our comms. We need to get a message out. I'm guessing the interference is a localized issue caused somehow by the damage done to their transmitter here... at least I'm hoping that's the case. If we can get out to a distance, I'm betting the satphone will work."

"Out on the ice? On foot?" Wilkins said.

"Not on foot; I've been told there's a basement storage area that's got two jet ski Skidoos, and maybe even some spare fuel for them. The folks in the wee tent there have been too scared to make an attempt for them."

"Ah," Wiggo said. "I see the problem. The bear will be out there waiting for us, won't it?"

Banks nodded.

"We need to take it down first. So here's the part you won't like. I'm proposing setting a trap. And what do traps need?"

"Bait," Wilkins said without thinking.

Wiggo laughed.

"Fastest volunteer in history. Don't worry, lad. We'll have your back."

Fifteen minutes later they were back in the ruin of the broken dome of Dome Three. Wilkins stood alone in the dark below the highest part of the structure. They'd cleared the tables and trestles away to the far side of the area and Wilkins felt tiny and exposed, knowing that he was in full view of anything that might be watching them from out there in the gloom. The other three members of the squad weren't visible, having taken cover in the shadows in strategic positions around the dome that the Captain had calculated would give them the best chance of catching the beast in crossfire.

"Remember," Banks had said to him, just before they left him alone, "we need it to come all the way inside; we don't want it to be able to give us the slip like the last time."

"I remember," Wilkins replied. "I'll also remember not to be so quick in opening my gob and putting my foot in it in future."

"Don't do that, lad. It's part of your charm," Banks replied with a laugh and clapped him on the shoulder. "Don't worry. We've got your back."

"It's not my back I'm worried about."

The Captain had laughed again at that, then had walked off into the shadows.

Wilkins had only been alone for a minute, but it felt like an eternity already. He couldn't see the others, and the only sound was his own breathing, the only thing moving the condensation of his breath. He switched on his gun light, raised the weapon, and aimed the beam out onto the ice, waving the light back and forth.

The response was immediate. A roar came from out in the night, then another. Wilkins kept moving the light from side to side, muttering under his breath.

"Come on then, big boy. Come to daddy."

Another roar pierced the cold night air, closer than the last. Wilkins peered into the gloom, trying in vain to make out any darker shadows in the murk. He waved the light in a wider arc, splashing a wash across the ice just outside the dome.

"What are you waiting for? Come on. Here I am. Dinner is served."

The next roar sounded like it came from right ahead of him. He raised his rifle barrel, shining the light above the ice, and in the same moment capturing his first sight of the bear. It was coming on at a gallop, another roar accompanying the sound of its feet on the ice. It sounded like a pounding drum.

Wilkins instinctively took a step backward before remembering his orders to stand his ground. He took aim, a slight tremor in the wash of light betraying him as the beast pounded closer. It came close enough for him to see two red, bleeding holes in its left shoulder, hits it had taken the last time, before it slowed and came to a halt standing outside the dome. It raised its head, sniffing the air.

"I'm right here," Wilkins said. "Come on, come and get me."

It pawed at the ground, making Wilkins think, not of a bear, but of a raging bull facing down a matador. In lieu of a red cape, he waved the light beam to and fro across its snout, seeing the ray reflected back at him in the huge, unblinking eyes. It snorted, waved a great paw in front of its nose as if confused, but came no closer. If he opened fire now he risked it escaping in the same manner it had previously.

He took a step forward towards the beast; the most difficult step of his life. It sniffed at the air again. He aimed his light directly at its left eye.

"Come on, laddie. What are you waiting for?"

It jerked, as if it had just taken a shock, raised its head and bellowed, the roar echoing around in the shattered dome, but still it would not come closer.

The stand off might have continued until one or the other of them succumbed to the cold had Davies not decided to take matters into his own hands.

He walked out of the darkness from Wilkins' right and stepped in front of the bear. He raised his rifle and fired a shot over its head.

"Come on then, fucker," he shouted. "Come and get it."

Wilkins heard Wiggo in the radio earpiece.

"For fuck's sake, lad. What are you playing at?"

The Captain's voice joined in.

"Davies. Get the fuck out of there. That's an order."

Davies wasn't listening. His weapon remained sighted on the bear.

"Come on," he shouted. "Let's see what you've got."

The bear jerked in a spasm as if it had been hit, raised its head, roared and leapt into an attack. Wilkins couldn't get a clear shot, his view blocked by Davies' body. He moved to one side and raised his own weapon, ready to back Davies up, but the Captain's voice in his ear stopped him in his tracks.

"Fall back, Wilko. That's an order. No sense both of you being in danger. Fall back and cover him."

He only just had time to retreat into the same shadows that Davies had emerged from; by then the bear was at the entrance to the broken dome, and still coming forward.

It roared, Davies screamed, and still it came on, still he didn't fire until it was almost on top of him. He put three quick shots into its head and tried to roll away but he'd left it too late. The beast might already be dead but its momentum kept it coming. It ran over the top of Davies, flattening him beneath it. It kept going another five yards before it realized it was dead and fell in a heap.

Wilkins was already on the move before it went still. He paused only long enough to put three rounds into the back of the huge head, then rounded a body the size of a family car, looking for Davies. The only sign of him was his left leg showing under the beast's bulk.

"Need a hand here," he shouted, and put his weight into trying to shift the stricken beast. He got nowhere until Banks and Wiggo finally joined him. They rolled the bear aside, revealing Davies' body.

"Oh no," Wilkins whispered.

Davies' face was a mask of blood. His right arm was broken, the butt of his rifle embedded in the wound where white bone showed. At first glance Wilkins was sure the man was dead, then Davies coughed, blood bubbling at his lips.

"Bloody thing's stoved in my ribs," he said in little more than a whisper.

Wilkins had to dig deep for his field training, and wasn't sure how good a job he was doing, but at least they got the broken arm stabilized and splinted and the bleeding from that wound stopped. The blood bubbles at Davies' mouth was another matter entirely; Wilkins was no expert, but he was pretty sure there was something actually broken in Davies' chest, perhaps even a punctured lung.

"You daft bugger. What did you think you were playing at?" he said.

Davies didn't reply, just continued to cough up blood.

"We need to get him back to the shelter in the other dome; he can't stay here lying in the cold," Wilkins said.

"You're right," Banks replied. "Wiggo… we need you over here."

Wiggo was only halfway paying attention; he was bent over the dead bear, moving fur aside at the base of its neck.

"Fuck me sideways," the sergeant said as he uncovered something. Banks stepped over to his side.

"What have you got, Sarge?"

"Trouble," Wiggo replied, and Wilkins saw him move the fur aside so they could all see.

It was small, no larger than a packet of cigarettes, and it was almost embedded in the bear's flesh so had been there for a while, a black box, a single small red light flashing in the center of the upper surface and a two-inch, pencil-thin aerial jutting up at the rear of it.

"What's this flashing mean, then, Cap?" Wiggo said "The beast's dead, but this thing's still sending."

"Or receiving. We've seen this kind of shite before," Banks said.

"Aye. Yon thing in the Yukon. Somebody's fucking about where they shouldnae be."

"Same as it ever was," Banks replied. "Dig it out and bring it with us. We cannae hang about out here any longer. Wilkins is right, we need to get Davies off this ice."

- MARGARET -

When the soldiers returned carrying a body Margaret thought the young black soldier was dead, but he groaned when they maneuvered him into the makeshift shelter.

She pointed at the empty cot bed; her work colleagues were all in theirs, although they had just been awakened by the soldiers' arrival.

"Put him in my bed, I'm not using it."

"That's a shame," the mouthy one from earlier replied, but she ignored him and helped get the wounded soldier into the bed.

 He cried out in agony as they put him down.

"Do you have any painkillers?" the Captain of the soldiers asked her. "He's going to need something."

"We've got some morphine in the medical cabinet," she said.

"Aye, that's just what he needs," the officer said sarcastically, but wouldn't offer anything further by way of explanation, merely sighed. "You'd better fetch it."

"You'll need my authorization before using anything from that cupboard," Collins said from his bed, showing no inclination to move from it.

"Well you know where you can stuff your authorization," she replied, and got a hand clap in reply from the mouthy soldier.

By the time she fetched the medical kit and returned, the three soldiers were at the tent entrance smoking and deep in conversation, studying something they passed between them. She pushed down her curiosity and headed inside; the man inside was what was important at the moment. When she entered the tent the injured man looked up at her imploringly.

"Have you got something for the pain?" he whispered, blood bubbling at his lips.

She showed him the morphine bottle.

"Fuck, that's what got me into trouble in the first place. That's all I need," he said through clenched teeth, but he didn't refuse it. She prepared a syringe, gave him an injection in his left arm and sat with him as they waited for it to take hold.

"What happened out there?" she asked.

"I fucked up again," he said. "I fucked up badly. That's what happened."

He showed her the broken arm, and touched gingerly at his chest, wincing as if even the slight touch brought pain with it.

"No, you *are* fucked up badly," Margaret replied. "And you're not out of the woods yet. You need to stay calm. Try to rest."

"I don't think I'll ever rest again. Not after this."

She was surprised to see tears in the man's eyes. She sat beside him and took his left hand, just as another wave of pain hit him. His white-knuckle grip threatened to squash her fingers, but she didn't let go or try to pull away.

"What's your name, soldier?"

"Davies," he said. "Just Davies. What's yours?"

"Margaret… Meg for short. Now lie still. Your pals have got you bandaged up well enough, but you don't look like you'll be going anywhere for a while."

"Pals? Aye, maybe," he said. "But maybe I've fucked that up too."

He coughed, and more blood bubbled at his lips, but the needle had done its job; his eyelids were drooping and his gaze took on the expected faraway look. He was almost under when he spoke again, so softly she hardly heard it.

"Tell them I'm sorry," he said, then the morphine took him away for a while.

She waited to make sure he was completely under then went out to join the soldiers at the entrance.

"How's he doing?" the Captain asked.

"He's pretty banged up. What happened to him?"

"He got flattened by a fucking enormous beastie," the mouthy one said. "And he shouldn't have been anywhere near it."

She got the full story from the Captain over a mug of coffee.

"So it was just a bear?" she asked when it seemed the story was done.

"A bloody huge one, aye. I suspect it's been genetically modified, or somehow specifically bred for a purpose. But it wasn't itself."

He showed her a little black box that still had bits of blood and fur stuck to it. He pointed at the back of his neck.

"The latest thing from some bioweapons division somewhere. Insert this at the top of the spinal column and Bob's your auntie's fancy man, you've got your very own wee remote controlled bundle of joy."

She examined the box, but, beyond recognising that it was both a transmitter and receiver, couldn't make head nor tail of it.

"Who would do such a thing?" she asked, handing it back.

"Mad scientists, bad scientists, and mad, bad scientists, from my experience at least."

She saw the way he was looking at her, and immediately her dander rose up.

"You don't think we did it ourselves, do you? We're all oceanographers and geologists here. This is way out of our field. Besides, some of those missing here were good...very good...friends of mine. What kind of monster do you take me for?"

He held up a hand.

"Just trying to cover all the eventualities," he said. "Don't take it personally."

"I can't see any other way to take it, can you?"

He smiled thinly.

"If not you, then who? Is there anybody else working in the area?"

"Not for hundreds of miles in any direction, as far as we know."

"As far as you know... aye, that'll hide a multitude of sins. That and the long night. But it certainly looks like somebody's been trying to queer your pitch," he said, tossing the small black box in one hand. "Let's see if we can get the flock out of here before they try something else."

"What's the plan?"

"Wilkins...that's the younger lad...and I will take out a pair of Skidoos, try to get out of range of whatever the fuck this interference is, see if we can call in some transport. Wiggins...he's the mouthy one you might have noticed...will stay here with you and the wounded lad."

"Well. I've got some bad news on that front," she replied. "There's a storm coming in. Should be here in no more than a couple of hours. Once that's over us, we're on our own for the duration."

"Same as it ever was," the officer said, as if to himself. "We'd best get a move on then."

He looked up.

"Wilko, you're with me. Wiggo, you watch the civvies here, and make sure Davies doesn't do anything else stupid."

The officer gave Meg a mock salute, and no more than a minute later he and the younger soldier were making their way back out of the dome.

The other soldier was already lighting up another smoke while standing just outside the tent.

"Wiggins, huh?"

"That'll be me."

She put out a hand.

"Margaret Paterson, formerly senior biologist in this fine establishment."

They shook hands.

Wiggins jerked a thumb at the entrance.

"How's he doing? Is he out of it?"

"You can go and see for yourself."

"Naw. If I get too close I'll just want to punch him, and that wouldnae be right."

"He said that he fucked up?"

"Aye, that he did," the soldier replied. "And he let the side down."

"And might have got himself killed doing it?"

"Aye, that too. Look after him for us, will you? He's a good lad if he's got his head on straight."

"What did he do that was so bad?" she asked, but still didn't get an answer. "Fuck it, I'll ask him myself."

"Do me a favor, lass," Wiggo said. "If you do get an explanation, let me ken, for I'm buggered if I can understand him right now."

She went back inside the tent. Her three companions were still bedded down in the dark corner, little more than dark shadows in the gloom, and it looked like they were all asleep once more. As for herself, sleep was the furthest thing from her mind; she was too wired, despite having been awake for more than forty-eight hours straight.

She sat on a camp chair by the stricken soldier's bedside. His breathing was fast and shallow, with blood bubbles still showing at his lips, but he was still out of it, which was probably for the best.

"Poor lad," she whispered. "What did you do to get yourself into this state?"

She was willing to wait for an answer.

- WILKINS -

The Skidoos were where they'd been told to expect to find them, and there was even light, if not much heat, in the cavernous basement under the domes. A diesel generator thudded rhythmically off against one wall, and a quick check showed the woman had been right earlier; the complex's fuel supply was getting dangerously low.

"Whatever we're going to do, we're going to need to do it fast," Banks said. "Come on, lad, let's see if we can figure out how to run these bikes."

It only took Wilkins and the Captain a matter of minutes to check the vehicles. They were ready to go and fully fueled, and their operation was so similar in style to a motorbike that Wilkins didn't foresee any great problem. It took them a few minutes longer to figure out how to open the doors to the ramp up and out onto the ice, but they eventually found the remote in the pocket of a jacket by the door, and were soon out in the open, moving along at speed, leaving the lights of the dome behind.

Cold bit at the skin below Wilkins' eyes, the only bit of him exposed between goggles and his fully zipped up parka. The Skidoo's handles felt like icy stone even through thick gloves, and the machine bucked and swayed in ways a motorbike never could. But if truth be told, he was happy to be out in the open. Since his wounding in the cellar in London he'd been especially wary of enclosed spaces. It wasn't that big a deal, at least that's what he told himself, but he'd felt it again in the pub in Orkney in the last mission. Driving the Skidoo after that felt like freedom, and he intended to enjoy it as much as possible, even in spite of the conditions.

He followed behind and to the left of the Captain, keeping out of the wake of hail-like ice thrown up by the bike. The headlights picked out the ice ahead for some twenty yards; beyond that there was only gloomy darkness. The sky had grown overcast since their earlier arrival and it felt like a change was in the air.

It was clear the Captain was in a hurry; this was no leisurely drive; he pushed his machine hard, heading for the horizon. Wilkins tried to keep up.

They pulled up several minutes later and cut their engines; the silence was sudden and like a heavy blanket falling around them. The light of the dome was only barely visible over to their right, there was a glitter of thin gray on the horizon far off beyond the dome; the only sign it was still daylight somewhere far away. All else was deep twilight. Wilkins almost jumped when the blaring honk of the station's siren cut through the night, three blasts then more silence.

"At least we're not going to get lost," the Captain muttered as he took out his satphone and switched it on. He sighed deeply seconds later before putting it away. "Still the same old shite. We'll need to go out farther. Are you game?"

"Whatever it takes, Cap, you know that."

"Good lad. Same as before, just follow my lead."

The Captain set off again, with Wilkins following. They hadn't gone far when Wilkins spotted something off to his left.

"Got something here, Cap," he said over the radio, at the same time flicking his headlights twice to get the Captain's attention. Both Skidoos came to a halt. The Captain dismounted and came over beside Wilkins.

"What is it?"

Wilkins turned his machine on an arc to illuminate what he'd seen; there was a disturbed area of snow and, beyond that, heavy caterpillar tracks heading off towards the horizon. There were also footprints, or rather, pawprints, the huge, almost circular marks unmistakable as those of the great bear.

"So somebody drove it here, dropped it off, then set it on the station using the wee box of tricks?" Wilkins said.

"Certainly looks that way, doesn't it?" Banks looked at the tracks, back towards the base, then back to the tracks. "I'm of a mind to see where these lead. Maybe they have better luck with their comms than we're having. Are you up for a wee side quest?"

Wilkins grinned.

"Just give the order, Cap."

Wilkins let the Captain bring his Skidoo round, and once again he followed. There were two sets of tracks, one coming, one going, both running parallel to each other and easy to follow. He was aware that they were probably making enough noise to give away their position, should anyone be listening for them, but the Captain seemed determined on this course of action, and Wilkins trusted his superior's instincts in these matters.

They traveled for almost twenty minutes. He was just starting to get concerned about having enough fuel for a return journey when the Captain came to a stop and killed his lights. Wilkins followed suit, got off the bike and joined Banks. The Captain was looking towards the horizon where a dim glow showed in the sky, the coronal blue of artificial lights.

Without a word, the Captain unslung his rifle and began walking. Again Wilkins followed.

The closer they got, the clearer it became that there was a large structure ahead, partially hidden in a dip in the ice. A wind was getting up, the cold was biting hard, but the Captain didn't slow. He led them to a ridge overlooking a bowl-shaped depression in the ground and they lay down flat, creeping forward on their elbows, and looked down over what looked almost comically like a circus; a large domed tent in the center and several long trailer-park style trailers around the exterior. A long ramp led up out of the enclosed area to their right; this was where the caterpillar tracks would have led had they followed them to the end. The light came from the tent, where a flap was open. Two heavily swaddled men led two huge white bears, larger even than the one the squad had recently killed. The beasts followed the men, as docile as a well trained dog, coming out of the tent to be led up into one of the trailers which looked to be more of an open cage than anything else.

The Captain tapped Wilkins on the shoulder, and indicated they should move round the depression to the left. They traversed the ridge quickly to be above a part of the encampment below that lay in deeper shadows. They went down the slope carefully; a single slip would send them sliding away into darkness with the risk of broken bones, or worse. It got even colder as they descended and Wilkins' legs started to remind him that they weren't quite ready for this kind of action. He pushed the thought away and gingerly followed the Captain down.

Once they reached bottom they began a survey of the nearest trailers; Wilkins knew they were looking for comms equipment, and its presence was immediately obvious by an array of masts and dishes atop a trailer some twenty yards to their right. It was also, unfortunately, close to the open tent flap, so better lit than the surrounding area. The Captain put a finger to his lips and motioned for Wilkins to follow as they crept through the shadows.

They reached the nearest edge of the trailer with no trouble, but had to fall back in the shadow behind it as the two well-wrapped men emerged from the tent. This time they closed the flap behind them; darkness fell across the complex. The men made their way to the trailer where they'd loaded the bears and spent several minutes hooking it up to a large caterpillar-tracked snowmobile. The snowmobile's lights came on, thankfully facing away from where Wilkins and the Captain were lurking, and the vehicle, with the caged bears in tow, headed off and away up the ramp.

And I can make a good guess where they're taking them.

The Captain moved as soon as the snowmobile went over the ridge and out of sight. He crossed quickly over the ground to a small window in the comms trailer and stood on tiptoe, peering in. As if satisfied with what he'd seen, he waved Wilkins forward, and signaled that Wilkins should watch the main tent. The Captain tried the door handle. It squeaked slightly, and both men tensed, but there was no answering sound. The handle turned fully, the door swung slightly open revealing a dimly lit room beyond filled with racks of servers, monitors and comms equipment. The Captain slipped inside.

Wilkins' legs were really starting to trouble him; this was the most activity he'd had since the thing on Orkney, and he'd needed a good few days rest after that shitshow; he wasn't looking forward to what the next few hours were going to bring.

It didn't look like he was going to be hanging around. The flap on the great tent shifted aside, a wash of light coming with it; Wilkins' position was suddenly exposed. He knocked twice softly on the trailer door to alert the Captain, then moved swiftly towards the shadows. He didn't make it.

As he reached the corner he heard it, a loud snuffling, like a dog sniffing at a lamppost; but this was something much bigger. He rounded the corner of the trailer and found himself face to face with another of the great bears. It loomed over him, its head a foot above him. It looked him up and down, as if puzzled by his presence. Wilkins was trying to ignore the wee voice inside him telling him to run when someone spoke at his back.

"They make wonderful killers," a man said in a thick Slavic accent, "but poor guard-dogs. I would put the weapon down if I were you, soldier, before I am tempted to let it have you."

"Do as he says, lad. We're blown."

Wilkins turned back to see the Captain, hands on his head, being led out of the comms trailer at gunpoint by two heavily swaddled men. The third man, the one who'd spoken, had a pistol aimed at the center of Wilkins' chest.

"What is it to be, soldier?" the man asked. "Me or the bear? Make your mind up. In case you haven't noticed, there's a storm coming in."

Wilkins handed over his weapon, put his hands on his head, and followed behind the Captain as they were led into the great tent.

- WIGGO -

The wind had got up outside the dome, its howl loud enough to overwhelm the honk of the warning klaxon. Snow spattered against the windows, showing only a shifting sheet of white. Wiggo had tried half a dozen times in as many minutes to reach the captain or Wilkins on their radios, but either they were deliberately maintaining radio silence, or they were out of range.

Or they're in deep shit.

He pushed that thought away; if the other two were in trouble, they were on their own, for there was no way Wiggo was going to be able to venture out of the dome on foot in the storm. Besides, he had civvies to babysit…civvies and a badly wounded soldier.

He still hadn't been able to face Davies. He'd spent the time since the others left standing outside the makeshift tent and chain smoking. It was bloody cold, and uncomfortable.

But not as uncomfortable as having to talk to the lad.

His anger was fading now, leaving behind resentment, disappointment, and more than a little guilt.

I should have seen it coming.

The longer he spent thinking about it, the more he thought he might understand. This job took its toll. They'd lost men before; Wiggo had lost good friends. His own drug of choice in such situations had always been booze and plenty of it.

But I never once got shitfaced on the job. There's the difference.

He was still trying to reconcile his conflicting emotions when the woman...Margaret she had said...came out of the tented area. She looked like she hadn't slept in days and her hair was a disheveled mess, but Wiggo knew better than to remark on either.

"I'm going to get some coffee on," she said. "Want some?"

"Does the Pope shit in the woods?" Wiggo replied, and was surprised to get a laugh.

"How's the others doing?" he asked as Margaret set about getting the camp stove working.

"George and the other two from here are sleeping. Your boy Davies is out for the count. It's probably for the best. If we don't get him to a hospital soon, he's not going to make it."

"Oh, and you're a medical doctor as well now, are you?"

"No, but I know a man who's given up hope when I see one. And so do you, I'm guessing?"

Hearing it put that starkly shook Wiggins hard. He left Margaret with the stove and went inside the tent, not knowing what he would say if Davies were awake. But the lad was still out, looking almost peaceful apart from the thin bubbles of blood that frothed at his mouth with every breath.

He went back out just in time to have a mug of hot coffee thrust in his hand.

"What did he do that was so bad?" Margaret asked softly, and just like that Wiggo's defenses came down and, over another smoke, she got the abridged story of the fuck-up in Patagonia, and Davies' decline into guilt and now, it seemed, morphine abuse.

"He's only a boy," Margaret said softly once the tale was done. "A boy that's seen too much."

"Aye. It comes with the territory though, and he's known that. If he'd only come to me…"

"Would you have listened? Or would you just give him some macho bullshit about sucking it all up?"

"You've been watching too many Clint Eastwood films, lass," Wiggo said.

"I'm not the only one," she answered, and pointedly went back inside without another word, leaving Wiggo to his coffee and smokes.

The weather was getting worse. He tried the squad radios again, but knew it was a forlorn hope. He could only pray that the two men had found shelter somewhere, for the thought of them lost out there on Skidoos was almost too much to bear.

Standing still wasn't doing anything to help with the seeping cold, so he walked the perimeter of the dome, checking the doors and generally trying to make work for himself to take his mind off anything else. To make matters worse, he was running out of smokes. Davies might have some, but that would involve a conversation he wasn't yet ready to have. So he walked, and he fretted while the weather continued to ramp up outside into a gale that wailed like a banshee.

He got back to the tent to find Margaret outside it. He had to almost shout to make himself heard.

"Is it always like this?" he said.

She laughed.

"No. Sometimes it snows."

Wiggo moved to the largest of the windows and again tried to peer out into the night. Blowing snow and glassy fragments of ice battered the glass. He couldn't see further than the length of his arm.

"They're in trouble, aren't they?"

The woman came to his side.

"If they got caught in it, they're in big trouble. But your captain looked as if he had his head screwed on right. He'll have seen it coming and found shelter."

"There's shelter?"

She nodded.

"Ice caves, hollows in the ground, maybe even old living quarters from previous expeditions; there's been a fair bit of activity in this area over the years; like Blackpool at the illuminations."

"Aye, but wi' fewer Scotsmen."

That got him another laugh, but it was a tired one.

"You need to get some kip, lass," he said. "You're running on fumes."

"And crap coffee… I know. But every time I close my eyes all I see is the running and the screaming and the blood. You know?"

"Aye, only too well. Davies did too, that's why he took to the hard stuff."

"How about you? How do you cope?"

She was echoing his own thoughts of earlier, and he almost didn't reply, and when he did he hid it behind a customary witticism.

"Booze, fags and loose women, in that order."

"Well then I might be able to help," she replied.

"Your tent or mine?"

"Not so fast, buddy. First things first. How do you take your ethanol?"

She led him to a tall double doored fridge.

"This is about all we could salvage, but I think I can rustle up a cocktail."

The mixture she made up was of orange juice and alcohol usually only used for experimental purposes, but it tasted pretty damn good to Wiggo, so much so that he was forced to turn her down when she offered more of the same.

"No, lass. I'm on duty. I'd be no better than Davies if I let myself get sloppy."

"How about a smoke then?" she said.

"Two out of three, my luck's changing for the better."

"In your dreams, buddy, in your dreams."

He was down to only five smokes left, but was happy to pass one over to her, and lit her up before taking one for himself. She smoked like somebody used to it, and saw his raised eyebrow.

"Five years quit, and now this. Just don't tell my mother; she'll go ballistic."

"I'll be the soul of discretion."

"Somehow, I doubt that," she replied with a grin.

This light flirting was certainly preferable to his previous gloomy brooding, and he was about to respond again when another sound rose up outside, clearly audible even above the wail of the wind.

Somewhere out there a great bear roared in rage.

- WILKINS -

The interior of the tent into which Wilkins and the Captain were led was awash with harsh lighting, too bright after the gloom outside. The perimeter around the tent's interior was lined with an array of large cages in which more of the great bears prowled; there must have been at least twenty of them, each as large if not larger than the one they'd shot earlier. The bears made no sound and, despite prowling in the cages, seemed to be unnaturally docile.

The tent itself was huge, covering the area easily the size of a football field, held up by large metal posts at six points and made of a thick material made to withstand anything the North Pole could throw at it. Whoever had authorized this operation clearly had plenty of money to throw at it.

There was further evidence of money having been spent in abundance as they got further inside. They were marched through a small township of heavy duty recreational trailers to a central hub that was a large dome made of opaque glass. Inside it was much like the one they'd left behind on the ice. This one had heat though, and it was a good thing too, for they were forced to divest their clothing and gear at gunpoint. Nobody had said more than a few words to them, except to bark orders.

Once stripped they were locked in a room little larger than a broom closet, wearing only their thermal underwear and their boots. It was warm enough that they weren't going to freeze, but it wasn't going to be exactly comfortable, and Wilkins' still recovering legs were already complaining about the rough treatment.

"What do you think, Cap? Russians?"

Banks nodded, but put a finger to his lips, and then pointed to his ears. Wilkins got the message; someone was probably listening in. It was going to be little more than name, rank and serial number time for the foreseeable future.

They each took a side of the room, but it didn't take long to take stock. It might well even have been a broom closet no more than ten minutes previously, for there was more than a hint of bleach or disinfectant in the air. But that was all that was present apart from the two men. The door was firmly locked, and air came in from a grille overhead, but even with the two of them putting their weight into it the grille itself would not be budged. They heard sounds wafting in from beyond; people working, machinery being moved, and a distant, but getting louder roar and whistle of wind.

Wilkins realized it might be for the best that they'd been captured.

Otherwise we'd have been caught too far from home base, in a storm, on Skidoos. That wouldn't have ended well.

But by the time half an hour had passed, any sense of gratefulness was washed away by the increasing bite of cold that seemed to seep in through the walls. Maybe it hadn't been a broom closet after all; now he was thinking more along the lines of a freezer compartment. The Captain's face looked gray and haggard, a bluish tinge at his lips; he looked the way Wilkins felt.

He almost let out a sigh of relief when there was a sound of a key in the lock, the door opened, and two rifle-carrying soldiers motioned that they should get out. For a brief instant Wilkins considered making a move for one of the weapons, but was stopped when Banks spoke softly.

"Not yet."

They allowed themselves to be herded towards the center of the dome, where another armed soldier opened a door to usher them into a well-appointed office. The first thing Wilkins noticed was the heat which seemed to emanate in waves from a large radiator that dominated one whole side of the room. His fingers tingled as feeling slowly began coming back to them.

The rest of the room was stocked with filing cabinets, two forty-eight inch screens, a couple of incongruous armchairs, and a small but rotund man who sat behind a large mahogany desk.

His gray, almost white hair with a matching beard. and the general stockiness of his manner, reminded Wilkins more than a little of the bears they'd seen out in the compound, but when the man looked up he smiled and his eyes twinkled.

He barked at his men in Russian, then turned back to address Wilkins and the Captain.

"I told them to disarm you, not strip you of your dignity," he said with a smile. "Come, we are all soldiers here. Clothing is on its way, as is coffee and your cigarettes. I would like you to be comfortable during your stay here."

"And what exactly is this place?" Banks asked.

"Like your place, this is a research center," the small man said. "As you have seen, experiments are currently in progress."

"I wouldn't call bloody murder an experiment."

"Wouldn't you? I would. And I have been expecting you, or someone like you for some time now."

"There are more of us," Banks said, 'at the research station. But you know that already, don't you?"

"Our research experiments require live animal testing in our case, I'm sorry to say," the Russian said, and the twinkle in his eye had gone as quickly as it had come. "You have your orders, I have mine."

"Under the Geneva Convention.." Banks started.

The Russian interrupted.

"Which we both, as soldiers, know is, how would you say it, bollocks. There are no conventions to help you here in the cold and dark. I am the only law here, and you would do well to remember it."

Two men…these ones didn't look like soldiers, but wore the uniforms of obvious workers…returned with clothing. It wasn't their own gear, but a set of fur-lined, sealskin hooded jackets and trousers with fur lined mittens attached to the arms with twine. As Wilkins pulled on the clothes he caught a musky odor from them, akin to that of a wet dog.

Once they were clothed Wilkins felt somewhat like a bear himself, being swaddled in a suit that was already proving to be too warm for the hot office.

"I should warn you," the Russian commander said, "our beasts are conditioned to follow and hunt certain scents. You are now a pair of walking snacks to them, so I would suggest you do not try to leave the relative comfort of the dome. Believe me, you would not last long."

Coffee was brought, and as promised, their cigarettes. The Russian offered a smoke of one of his, a plain box with capital letters L and D. Captain Banks declined.

"Thank you, no. I've had those before. I wouldn't call them a pleasure."

The Russian laughed.

"A dubious one at best, I agree, but I am too far gone in my addiction to notice."

When the coffee was served the Russian put a splash of vodka in his from a decanter on his desk, but pointedly didn't offer it around; his hospitality only stretched so far. It did however, seem to make him even more voluble. He motioned Wilkins and the Captain to the armchairs. Wilkins unbuttoned the sealskin jacket to the waist; he was already starting to sweat inside it.

The Russian waited till they were seated, lit up a smoke, and addressed the Captain.

"How are things at the research station?" he asked, almost conversationally.

"Mostly dead," the Captain replied. "And that's all you get out of me. Coffee and smokes are all well and good, but I don't spread my legs for them."

"Just tell me one thing. The bear? Did you kill it?"

Banks nodded.

"That was unfortunate. You will have found our latest surprise then?"

"No surprise to us. Where did you get it? Siberia or the Yukon?"

Banks had scored a point; Wilkins saw the shock in the Russian's face although the man masked it quickly under pretense of getting another smoke lit.

"I see I was right in bringing you here," he said. "That was supposed to be a secret. I will know how you knew it."

"Well, you won't hear it from me," Banks answered.

"You said you have other people, maybe still alive at the research station, no?"

"Captain John Banks, 635780," the Captain replied.

The Russian laughed.

"My, you have been in service nearly as long as me. But clam up if you must, it is of no matter. I have ordered that your station be completely destroyed. The beasts are on their way there now, and you are powerless to stop them."

- MARGARET -

There had been no recurrence of the roaring for the last twenty minutes, but that only made things worse; her mind was working overtime, imagining the thing on the prowl out there in the snow. She envied her workmates their sleep. All three were still out for the count. The young soldier, Davies, however, was showing signs of coming up into consciousness and given the distress showing in his face, it wasn't going to be a happy wakening.

She went to his side and put a hand to his forehead; heat radiated off him, accompanied by a sickly smell. She wondered if he'd soiled himself, but that wasn't anything she felt like investigating too closely. His eyelids fluttered and he looked up at her, his gaze unfocused.

"Sarge?"

"No, hold on, I'll get him."

The sergeant was outside the tented area, for once not smoking, but studying the small black box the Captain had shown to Margaret earlier.

"Your boy's awake. He's asking for you. You should go to him."

"I should kick his arse from here back to Glesca, that's what I should do," he muttered. "But there's something he might be able to help us with."

She followed him back into the tent.

Davies looked up, not at the sergeant, but at Margaret.

"Have you any more of that stuff?"

Wiggins butted in.

"Even if she has, you shouldnae even be thinking about it."

Davies coughed, fresh blood showing at his lips.

"I'm broken, Sarge. Broken deep inside. I can feel it grating, can feel things slipping away that shouldnae be moving at all. I'm done up like a kipper."

Margaret saw that the sergeant had a caustic remark in mind, so put a hand on his shoulder to stop him, and got her oar in first, speaking to Wiggins.

"You said there was something the lad could help us with?"

The sergeant appeared to come to a decision. He showed Davies the small black box.

"Do you remember this shite?"

Davies nodded, and coughed again, moaning in pain.

"I do, Sarge. Where did you get this one?"

"Off yon great beastie you let run over you. We need to find out where the controls are coming from. You managed it afore. Are you fit enough to do it again?"

Davies suddenly looked like an eager puppy, his youth showing through the pain that had ravaged his face.

"Just fetch my laptop from my kit," he said. "I've probably still got the algorithm Wilko and I worked up the last time."

"You shouldn't be doing anything at all but resting," Margaret said, but Wiggins brushed her concerns aside.

"If I know the Captain, he's already found what we're looking for. And he might be in trouble."

"Fetch that bloody laptop and let's be about it then," Davies replied. "I've only got one good arm, but that's all I need for this."

"There's the soldier I've been looking for," Wiggins said. "I ken he was still in there somewhere."

Wiggins fetched Davies' laptop then went back outside for another smoke. Margaret helped the injured man up into a reclining position where he could use the computer. It was obvious that it took him a huge effort just to get that far, but he brushed her away when she tried to put him back down.

He showed her the small black box.

"This is important," he said.

"Well, I know your sergeant thinks so."

"No, this is important, to me. It's redemption. You ken the word?"

She nodded.

"I know it."

"I wonder if you understand it though. I fucked up. This is my way back. Some of it, anyway. Now let me work."

It was only a few minutes later that he looked up.

"All done," he said. "Get the Sarge in here, would you. I think I've earnt some more of that dream juice."

When the sergeant came in, Davies greeted him with a thumbs-up, but even that brought with it more blood at his mouth and a wince of pain.

"The signal's coming from a spot about ten miles west," Davies said. "But there's more, Sarge. I can piggy-back on it."

"You can what?"

"I can send a message back the way it came. And better than that, I'm through their firewall, piece of shit that it was. I can get a message out. I just need you to tell me what to say."

"A message? To Lossiemouth?"

"Straight to the Colonel's desk if I've got it right. Should pop up on his laptop."

"Then let's hope the auld duffer isnae asleep on the job. Make it so, lad. Call in the cavalry."

While the soldiers were confabbing over the text of their proposed message, Margaret filched Davies' cigarettes and lighter from the open kit bag and helped herself to one. She refused to even consider it a guilty pleasure. No, this was more along the lines of a necessary evil. She backed out of the tent and stood in the gloom of the laboratory. Snow and ice continued to lash against the windows, and she felt the dome shift slightly below her. She had told the sergeant that there might be shelter out on the ice for the lost squaddies, but in her heart she was beginning to think they were already lost. Their only hope seemed to lie with the message now being attempted on Davies' laptop.

I hope to Christ they know what they're doing.

What few lights were turned on flickered, dimmed, and brightened again. By her count they were now on their last tank of fuel for the generator.

Once that's gone, we're as good as dead in a matter of hours.

Her hands trembled as she lit up a smoke, but she didn't even get time to take a draw. Even as the lighter flared on, a bellowing roar rent the air, and the far side of the dome from her caved in with a crash. A gale blew in through a hole that was almost immediately filled with the head and shoulders of a massive white bear.

Its gaze fell on her. It raised its head and roared, launching itself into an attack.

- WIGGO -

"Here goes nothing."

Davies hit the send command on his laptop. As if in response there was an almighty crash from outside the makeshift tent, which immediately billowed and snapped around them as if it was caught by a rush of wind.

"What the fuck is this now?" Davies said.

Wiggo didn't think, acting on pure instinct as he stood away from the cot, picked up his rifle and threw himself out of the tent. All in all it took him maybe five seconds. He was still almost too late. The woman stood between Wiggo and the headlong rush of another of the great bears. It saw Wiggo and roared again. He might have had a clear shot right down its throat if he wasn't impeded. He considered, for a fraction of a second, taking the shot anyway, then adrenaline fueled his immediate decision.

He tackled the woman around the waist, driving with his legs to take her away and out of the line of the bear's attack. They both rolled aside and Wiggo turned, weapon already raised, just in time to see the bear barrel right on top of the makeshift tent, trampling and roaring, great paws ripping material to rags and throwing cots and their occupants high in the air. Its head went down and came back up with blood coating its snout from nose to ears.

"Davies!" he shouted.

He heard gunfire, somewhere beneath the bear.

The wee bugger is still alive.

Wiggo put three quick rounds into the bear's flanks. It was like shooting a brick wall. The beast barely flinched, and kept rooting among the debris of the collapsed tent. Two more shots came from somewhere on the other side of the beast.

"Hold on, lad," Wiggo shouted. "I'm coming."

He took a running jump, landing on the bear's back and clambering up to stand on top of it. He almost lost his balance but was able to bend forward and grab a handful of its fur with his free hand and stay upright. The bear took no notice of him, fully intent on getting at Davies. Wiggo saw a muzzle flash at the beast's front end, then heard a high, wild scream. The bear shook as if hit by a shock, and roared, almost deafening in the confines of the dome.

"I'm coming, lad," Wiggo shouted again, once again only barely managing to keep his balance as the bear bucked below him. Once he was sure of his footing he stepped up high between its front shoulder blades and looked for the black box. He saw the stem of the aerial jutting out and focused on that. As he took aim he caught a movement in his peripheral vision; Davies, standing up front, blood pouring from a huge gash from sternum to waist, guts rolling out of him but still with his rifle raised, aimed at the beast's head.

They fired in unison, Wiggo using the opportunity to also blast the black transmitter to small pieces. The bear reared up on its back legs, throwing Wiggo off backwards, gave out one last roar, this one filled more with pain than rage, then fell forward, hitting the dome floor with a thud that shook the whole structure.

Wiggo rolled away and onto his feet, immediately looking for Davies. The lad was nowhere to be seen. He clambered, frenzied now, over the beast's body, hoping against hope that the wound the lad had taken wasn't as bad as a quick glance had made it look. A gust of wind at his back brought a wave of snow with it, obscuring his view further. Cold bit hard at him, but he hardly noticed, his whole focus on reaching Davies.

"Talk to me, lad," he shouted, but didn't get a reply.

He went up across the beast's back and looked down. Its snout lay across Davies' thigh. The lad was feebly trying to get out from under it. Then Wiggo saw the wound. It was even worse than he'd feared. Indeed, it was a bloody miracle Davies was still alive, for he had been opened almost from groin to neck.

Wiiggo leapt down to the man's side. The bear's body was now providing them with a modicum of protection from the weather, but it wasn't going to help them for long.

Wiggo heaved the bear's head off Davies' legs and bent to the man's side.

Davies looked up at him and smiled thinly. Blood came in a gush as he spoke.

"There's no pain, Sarge. It disnae hurt a bit. How do you like my solution to the Kobayashi-Maru?"

"I'm no' keen on it all, lad," Wiggo replied, and took Davies' left hand between both of his. Margaret was clambering among the wreckage of the tent, calling out the names of her colleagues, but Wiggo only had eyes for Davies. He was going fast.

The injured man struggled to speak. Wiggins spoke softly.

"Quietly, lad, you'll do yourself an injury."

Davies managed a thin smile, and managed to speak, his voice little more than a whisper.

"Sorry, Sarge."

The life went out of his eyes, leaving only the all-too-familiar china-doll stare of the dead.

Wiggo patted the dead man's hand.

"Me too, lad. Me too," he said, and let Davies' hand fall.

Margaret had stopped sifting through the rubble and was standing, looking down but not seeing. When Wiggo rose he saw the pool of gore at her feet. It might have been the remains of one body, or three, it was too badly torn to be sure.

"They're all dead," the woman said, fresh tears rolling down her cheeks and starting to freeze.

Wiggo wiped away tears of his own that he hadn't known were there. His first thought was to find shelter; the wind howled and raged through the broken wall of the dome, and snow was quickly filling in the floor space around them.

"Lass," he said, then louder when she didn't reply. "Lass, we need to get out of here. Is there anywhere at all we can go?"

She only took note of him when he held her arm.

"They're all dead," she said again.

"Aye. And so will we be if we don't get the fuck out of this wind. Where can we go?"

She touched at her eyes and it was as if the feel of the ice on her lashes brought her, a little way at least, back to the world.

"The basement. It's our only hope. There's light, and the generator, Some heat, maybe."

Wiggo retrieved Davies' weapon, had one last look at the body, then turned away.

"There's nowt we can do for them now. A proper send off will have to wait. The basement it is. Lay on MacDuff, and don't spare the horses."

They nearly didn't make it; the strength of the wind was such that it took both of them to open the basement door, and even then it took most of Wiggo's rapidly fading reserves to keep it open long enough for both of them to get through. His hands felt like lumps of cold stone, his left eye was frozen shut, and his legs were telling him it was time for a nice lie down. But finally they were out and let the basement door slam shut behind them with the sound of finality.

He took a few seconds to recover his breath then looked around. The basement seemed to run under almost the whole area of the dome above, a cavernous room with minimal light. There was a modicum of heat...it wasn't what you could call warm, but it was positively tropical compared to the Arctic hell above them. A generator chundered in the far corner. Two empty bays showed where the Skidoos had sat earlier, and a track led up a ramp to a, thankfully closed, bay door.

Margaret stood, slumped against the wall, her gaze on something far away. He saw she was still clutching tightly to a now slightly mangled pack of cigarettes and a lighter. He prized both from her grip. She hardly noticed.

Shock. I've got to get her moving, get her to focus on something else.

"We need to take stock," Wiggo said. "Food, water and heat, that's what we need. I'll check the genny, you have a shufti around the room."

He lit two cigarettes and handed one to her. He had to hold her hands steady before she could grip it properly, but the act of smoking seemed to bring her another notch back towards herself, and she nodded when he asked if she was okay. He didn't give her time to stop and think, but sent her on a hunt around the room while he investigated the generator.

She hadn't been exaggerating when she'd said fuel supplies were low; there was only one tank of diesel left feeding to the generator. The only point in their favor now was that they were currently in the only room left to heat and light, but that was a small mercy at best, for he could feel the cold already starting to leech down from the room above despite the generator's best efforts.

Apart from the diesel he found a hefty ice-axe and two twenty-litre containers of gasoline for the Skidoos, one full, one half-full. He met Margaret back at the center of the room. She had a four-litre bottle of water at her feet, and two small packets of salted peanuts in her hand.

"Found the nuts in one of the jacket pockets by the door. Thank the Lord for squirrels."

No sooner had she spoken than the tears were flowing again. Wiggo stepped forward, thinking to embrace her, but she backed away.

"No, I'm fine. I just need some time, you know?"

"You and me both, lass."

He was about to light another cigarette when there was a change in the noise up above. The wind was still howling, the foundations of the dome, what was left of it, still rocking and rolling, but there was something else too. It took him a few seconds to identify it, but once he knew what it was there was no doubt.

Something was moving about up there, despite the storm. Something big and heavy. Something about the size of another of the great bears.

- WILKINS -

After their brief meeting with the Russian commander, Wilkins and the Captain were escorted under armed guard back to their cell. At least they were warmer now, and had their smokes, but there was little good to be said for their situation.

"Bastards," Banks said after a while in quiet smoking. "Fucking bastards."

Wilkins didn't know whether to reply, given their earlier admonishment about keeping schtum, but the Captain seemed past caring on that score.

"If you're worried about them listening in, don't be. Fuck them, their mothers and the horses they rode in on. We're getting out of here, lad, and they're going to regret they ever fucked with us."

"How did they get an operation this size all the way out here without anybody noticing?"

"Because they're sneaky bastards, that's how," Banks replied. "I'm guessing the signal jamming is coming from here, probably from yon trailer. I didn't get enough time with their equipment to find out, but they've got enough kit here to keep a small country running."

"You didn't get a message out?"

The Captain shook his head rather than reply.

"I didna get enough time. We're on our own. And we need to do something about it real soon. You heard the man...they're aiming to destroy our base completely. Our friends need us."

Saying it proved easier than doing anything about it though. There was no egress from the cell, and no sign of anyone coming to check on them.

Wilkins sniffed at the sealskin suit. It was worse now in the confines of the small room.

"Why would anybody want to train bears as an attack force? Isn't it all a bit medieval?"

"That's Russians for you," Banks said, but the Captain wasn't paying attention. Wilkins saw him looking at the ceiling.

"Could it really be that easy?" Banks muttered to himself.

Wilkins looked up, and didn't see what the Captain had noticed, until the officer raised his lighter and flicked it on. They could now see through the grille overhead. The Captain had placed the lighter under what looked like a sprinkler head.

"Best get your hood up, lad. If I'm right we're about to get a soaking."

Wilkins barely got time to raise his hood before a klaxon alarm kicked in at a deafening volume and a spray of water gushed from the sprinkler.

"Get ready, lad, they'll be coming," Banks said. "You take the left, I'll take the right."

"What if there's more than two of them?"

"Then this is a fucking stupid plan."

The lock clicked and the door swung open seconds later. Wilkins went through it in a waist high dive that would have made his old rugby coach proud, had just enough time to see an astonished gape on the face of the soldier standing directly in front of them, then they were both rolling on the compound floor. The element of surprise gave Wilkins the advantage; he rolled on top of the man, grabbed his opponent's head with both hands and slammed him back onto the ground with all the weight he could muster behind it. The man's eyes fluttered, rolled back in his head, and he stayed down when Wilkins rolled off him. He turned to see that the Captain had dispatched his own man with brisk efficiency.

The men both bore rifles, and had handguns and ammo in belts at their waists. Wilkins and the Captain took just enough time to divest them of the weapons. The klaxon was still blaring, and the area around them was a hive of activity of men running and shouting. As of yet nobody was paying them any attention. They lugged the two would-be guards back into the trailer and shut them inside.

"They're going to get wet," Banks said. "At least mine is; I think you might have killed yours."

"No less than he deserved," Wilkins replied.

The Captain clapped him on the shoulder.

"Let's get out of here. It's high time we got back to the others."

They slipped out of the dome keeping to shadows as much as possible and took a hiding spot between two of the large trailers. The klaxon shut off abruptly, but the frenzy of activity continued for several more minutes before everything fell quiet.

A voice came over a tannoy system; the Russian commander, and he did not sound happy.

"Well played, gentlemen," he said. "But you have nowhere to go; your base is destroyed and the storm still rages. Give yourselves up. I guarantee you, you will be better with me rather than my new guard dogs. You don't think I gave you those suits out of the kindness of my heart, do you? They have your scent, they have your trail. I estimate less than five minutes before they have you. I am in my office should you wish to talk."

The Captain tapped Wilkins on the shoulder and indicated that they should be on the move. Wilkins followed as they quickly made their way behind the trailers to where they had a view of the wall of the outer tent. Two armed guards stood at the exit where they'd been brought in, facing into the tent. There wasn't going to be any way to sneak past them. The outer tent was rippling and billowing and the whistle and roar of the wind was loud here. Wilkins felt the cold already begin to bite at his hands and face.

Surely the Captain doesn't intend us to go out in this without goggles?

He wasn't given time to ask.

Banks dispatched the guards with two shots, both to the head. They went down before they knew what hit them and moments later Wilkins and the Captain were running across the open floor space, wondering whether their next step might not be their last, expecting at any instant a bullet between their shoulder blades.

No attack came.

They quickly ransacked the guards for what they could find; as well as a thick vest for each of them to go under the sealskin jackets, they both got goggles and another handgun each. The Captain also got a long-bladed knife in a sheath that fitted on his belt.

Wilkins quickly put on the vest; it was a loose fit, but he wasn't about to complain. He stowed the weaponry as well as he could in the pocket of his sealskin suit.

"What's the plan, Cap?"

"We're heading for one of yon caterpillar trucks," he said, "and we're getting the fuck out of here. Simple enough?"

"Works for me."

"And keep your eyes peeled for those fucking bears. The wee man seems awfy keen on seeing us get eaten. Let's disappoint him."

They lifted the flap and headed out into the storm.

The wind was in their faces straight away, almost blowing them backwards, and even wearing the goggles it was nigh near impossible to see much farther than five yards ahead. But the Captain seemed to know where he was going, and Wilkins followed him, taking care to stay close; if he lost sight of the man in the snow he might be blundering about lost until the cold got him.

A darker shadow loomed ahead. At first he thought it must be the snowmobile but then it came closer. A great bear stood directly in their path, not moving, but watching them like a guard dog might watch its sheep. Wilkins moved to raise his rifle but the Captain stopped him with a hand on the barrel.

"Don't kill it yet. I may have a plan," the Captain said, leaning close to shout in Wilkins' ear to be heard above the wind. "You go left, I go right. Not too far, stay in sight, but let's see if we can confuse it. And if you get a clear shot, take out the black box rather than the bear."

The bear raised its head and sniffed the air.

We're lucky we're downwind.

It ambled forward with no great urgency. Wilkins got a clearer idea of the size of the beast; its head, even though dropped down between the shoulder blades, was still high above Wilkins, eight feet off the ground at a guess.

Wilkins took a step left. At the same time the Captain moved right. The bear stopped and swung its head from side to side, looking first at Wilkins, then at the Captain. Banks, to Wilkins' amazement, threw his hands high in the air, waving the rifle at arm's length above him. Wilkins only understood this part of the plan when the bear turned towards the movement and raised its head; Wilkins had a clear shot at the black box at the nape of its neck.

He didn't need to wait for an order. Even as the bear turned fully to move towards the Captain, Wilkins swung his weapon up, took aim and put two quick shots at the black box. The first missed by inches, bringing a roar of pain from the bear. The second blew the box into little more than scattered fragments of plastic and circuitry. The bear reached back with a huge claw, clawing at this latest grievance, but the Captain wasn't done yet.

The Captain again astonished Wilkins. He didn't drop to take a shot at the confused bear, but fired his weapon into the air above the beast's head to get its attention, then, once its gaze fixed on him, turned and ran, not in the direction of the caterpillar trucks that had been their destination, but back towards the tent.

He saw Banks look back to ensure the bear had got the message. It was lumbering towards him, picking up speed, ensuring that he had to run full pelt. Wilkins could only watch, open-mouthed, as the Captain reached the tent flap. The bear was almost on him. At the last second he rolled aside. The bear's momentum kept it going. It barreled through the flap, ripping a huge swathe of material from the tent. Almost immediately startled shouts and then screams came from inside, heard even above the wind.

The Captain dusted himself off and trotted back to Wilkins' side.

"That should keep them busy for a bit."

Five minutes later they were ensconced inside one of the caterpillar-tracked snowmobiles. It took a further minute for Wilkins to hotwire the ignition, and then they were off and away, the Captain driving.

Wilkins took one look back at the encampment as they went up the snow ramp out of the hollow. The swirling snow made it hard to see, but the bear had ripped a large, clear hole in the tent and the storm was swirling in to try and fill it. He guessed everybody was still busy with the now-rogue bear, for no one came out to wave them goodbye.

- MARGARET -

It only took the great bear a matter of minutes to find the door to the basement. Margaret clearly heard it rooting and snuffling on the other side.

"It knows we're here," she said dully.

"Aye, either it, or whoever's controlling it. It'll get in."

"How do you know?"

"I've got years of experience of this for one thing," Wiggins said. "And for another, I watch films. The beastie always gets in. You ken that…"

All Margaret wanted to do was lie down and go to sleep, to wake up in a world where there were experiments to be done and everybody was still alive to do them. Her earlier experience in fleeing the initial assault was now overlain in her head with the too-fresh sight of her dead companions, and of that poor young soldier, split from neck to groin and still trying to be brave. She felt hot tears rise in her eyes and brushed them away.

"But how can it know we're here? Who's doing this to us?"

"We can only hope the Captain and the wee lad have found out," Wiggins replied. "But for now, we've got other things to worry about."

"Like what?"

"Like surviving the next five minutes. Don't go soft on me now, lass. I need you sharp."

She gave him a mock salute.

"Aye, aye, sir."

"That's better," Wiggins replied.

The bear continued to snuffle on the far side of the door. It was only a matter of time before it put its weight into it. Seconds after that it would be on them.

"We could get out via the ramp while it's up above," Margaret said.

Wiggins shook his head.

"That wouldnae do us any good at all. All it would get us is out in its territory, running blind in a storm. Fighting a bear in an enclosed space is probably better than fighting one where it's got room to get at you easier."

That made a certain kind of sense, but Margaret was struggling to get her brain in gear; images of the dead kept bubbling up, threatening to overwhelm her. Wiggins had said something, and she'd missed it.

"No time for wool gathering, lass," he said. He thrust one of the Skidoo fuel containers at her. "Pour this around the door, under it if you can manage."

"We can't start a fire in here," she said.

"Worried about the insurance, are we?" Wiggins replied. He had already moved over to the ramp, walked up to the outside door and was pouring fuel all across its base.

"This is just a wee back up plan, if all else fails."

"I'd say everything has pretty much failed already."

"Aye. But you don't have my built in advantage."

"What's that?"

"I'm a Glaswegian. We embrace failure. Then we kick it in the baws."

"Does that beast even have any?"

"If it does, I'll be having them for breakfast."

The door creaked loudly; the bear was putting its weight against it. Wiggins handed Margaret a Zippo cigarette lighter.

"The beast's going to find it a tight squeeze getting in, if it's as big as the others. That'll slow it down, give me a chance to get a headshot. If I don't slow it, flick this on and throw it under its belly. With any luck the flames will get contained and we'll have barbecue for supper."

"And if it doesn't work?"

"Then I guess it'll be my baws that are on the menu."

The door bent visibly, the hinges squealing.

"Showtime," Wiggins said, and pushed Margaret behind him as the door burst open.

She saw immediately that the man had been right about the bear finding it a tight squeeze; the door fell in with a clatter and bang and the beast's frustrated roar filled the room as it tried to enter and only made it as far as its shoulders. Wiggins didn't hesitate. He pumped three shots into the bear's face. It reacted as if electrocuted, throwing its bulk from side to side in a frenzy. The walls on either side of the doorway caved under the pressure, and what was left of the dome above began a slow collapse into the basement. The bear kept writhing, roaring in rage as it tried to force itself into the room. Snow began to whirl in from above.

"Just die, you bastard," Wiggins shouted, waited for it to roar again and put three shots down its throat. It fell in a heap in the doorway, but the damage had been done. The whole side of the dome above had fallen in around the bear, letting the storm rage through the room.

"We need to get out of here," Margaret said.

"And where?" Wiggins replied. "I'm open to suggestions, lass. But our options are limited here. What we need to do is buy ourselves some time and hope the cavalry rides over the hill."

"We could burn the bear?"

"I doubt that would help much," Wiggins said as the wind went up a notch and snow started to fill the basement around them. She saw him look at the ice-ax, and back to the bear.

"You have an idea?" she asked.

"Aye. But you're not going to like it. Given your quip earlier about stormtroopers I know you've seen the first movie. But have you seen 'The Empire Strikes Back'?"

- WILKINS -

The snowmobile made slow time through the storm, and Wilkins couldn't fathom how the Captain knew which direction to take, for all he could see ahead of them was a white sheet of swirling snow. The wind buffeted them, causing the vehicle to lurch and rock alarmingly. They'd passed their two discarded Skidoos some time ago; Wilkins had already said a silent prayer of thanks that they weren't trying to get back on the bikes. The snowmobile might be struggling, but at least they were inside and out of the wind.

The only other thing in their favor was that any pursuit would be in the same storm, in the same situation.

"It's not a pursuit I'm worried about right now," Banks said as Wilkins lit them both a smoke. "It's what's ahead of us that concerns me right now. Yon commander said that they'd mounted an operation to destroy our research station. If that's the case, I'd expect them to be still there or thereabouts when we get there. It's going to be tricky, given the storm."

Wilkins tried to peer out, but only succeeded in giving himself a headache. The forward movement of the snowmobile, into the wind, meant that the snow was coming at them as if from out of a funnel, like a warp-drive effect in a space movie, but with less of the exhilaration. The headlights were strong in these vehicles, but still not strong enough to penetrate more than ten yards ahead at a time.

"If we can't see them, they can't see us," Wilkins said.

"I'm not so sure about that, lad," the Captain replied. "I saw their tech, remember? I'm damn sure they're not lumbering about blind."

He waved a hand at the myriad rows of buttons and screens in front of the driving position. "Fuck knows what any of this shite does, and we've no time to waste experimenting."

He tapped at one dial. "All I know is that this is a compass, and we're heading mostly east. Knowing our luck tonight we'll drive right past the place in this shite."

They drove in silence for several minutes, then Wilkins saw something ahead.

"Tracks, Cap. Fresh ones at that."

"Then we've got a trail to follow. Keep those eyes peeled, lad. The game's afoot."

Less than a minute later Wilkins saw something through the snow ahead. The Captain saw it at the same moment. He killed the snowmobile's headlights and shut off the engine. They looked out at the dim red lights, obviously the rear lights of another snowmobile.

"If they've seen us, we'll ken soon enough," Banks said, unslinging his rifle.

Wilkins followed suit and they sat there in the swirling darkness, waiting to see if an attack would be forthcoming.

Nothing happened.

"I guess they're looking the other way," Banks said with a thin grin. "Are you up for a wee walk, lad?"

They exited the snowmobile on either side. Wilkins could barely see the Captain in the swirling snow. Their only point of reference was the dim glow of lights some twenty yards ahead. Wilkins fell in behind the Captain, rifle in hand and ready should anything come at them.

They moved swiftly up towards the lights. The snow whipped hard in their faces and it was impossible to see anything at all to either side. They focused on the lights, and were soon close enough to see that it was another snowmobile, the twin of the one they'd just departed. He saw the Captain motion that Wilkins should take the right-hand side. The Captain went left while Wilkins sidled along the side of the vehicle. If there was anyone inside it, they weren't paying any attention to their rear for Wilkins was able to quickly reach the door at the front. He kept low. All he could see inside was a darker shape behind the heavily tinted glass. He held his position and waited for the Captain to give him a signal.

It wasn't long in coming. Wilkins heard a muffled cry of surprise from inside the vehicle. Two shots rang out on the far side, the passenger door above Wilkins opened and a figure loomed over him. Wilkins saw a handgun in the process of being raised in his direction. He didn't need any encouragement. He put two shots into the man's chest and the Russian fell arse over it onto the snow, dead before he got cold.

The Captain cried out from the other side of the vehicle.

"All clear."

Wilkins made his way round the front of the snowmobile and joined the Captain who stood over another dead Russian.

"Fucker wasn't very friendly," Banks said.

"No, nor mine either, Cap."

They looked inside the now empty snowmobile. The engine was running, with a key in the ignition.

"Can you drive one of these buggers, Wilko?" Banks asked.

Wilkins had a look at the controls and nodded.

"Piece of pish, Cap. Race you back?"

"Give me time to bring the other one up. I'll pass by and go first."

"And what if we meet one of the yon bears?"

"Then we run the fucker over. Twice, to make sure."

Five minutes later Wilkins was following the Captain's lead, sitting three yards behind the lead snowmobile. It appeared that the snow might be lessening, for there was no difficulty in keeping the front vehicle's lights in sight. They left the Russians lying in the snow. They were dead. They weren't going anywhere.

- WIGGO -

It took Wiggo almost a quarter of an hour to hollow out enough room inside the carcass of the dead bear for both of them to fit; it had involved mainly hacking through belly fat to get at the guts, then pulling and tugging at the hefty intestines to drag them out. By the time he was done he was coated in gore from ankles to neck. He was also getting cold, despite the effort, for the storm was pushing cold air and snow ever deeper into the partially collapsed room, and what little heat the generator was still providing was being sucked away far too fast. He worked quicker, grunting with the effort as he tugged the last of the bloody mess out of the belly cavity and tossed it away to join a pile that had replaced the parking area of the Skidoos with a butcher's charnel house.

"Shit, it stinks worse than Maryhill on bin day," he said once he was satisfied. "But it'll do the job."

He motioned Margaret forward. She had been watching the whole process in dumbfounded amazement, and her face showed her disgust at the very idea being proposed.

"If you think I'm climbing in there, think again," she said.

Wiggo grinned.

"Don't worry, lass, you'll have company. Now are you getting in nicely or do I have to use my charm? It's make your mind up time, now or never..."

She stopped him from going on.

"I get it. It's just..." she waved a hand at the carcass. "We're about to climb inside a giant, dead, polar bear."

"Well, we wouldnae try it if it was alive, would we?"

That got him a smile, a thin one at best, but something to be going on with. He held open the gaping lips of the bear's wounded belly.

"Ladies first."

A fresh gust of bitter wind seemed to strengthen her resolve. She stepped over and tried to clamber inside the bloody cavity. It was an ungainly process, not helped by the fact that she got a foot caught in some of the exposed fatty tissue. In the end Wiggo expedited matters by putting both hands on her backside and giving her a shove. Her startled scream was muffled as she disappeared fully inside the belly of the beast. Then, before she had a chance to complain, he took up the two rifles, slung them over his shoulder, and squirmed in alongside her. He pulled the lips of the wound almost closed behind him; they were now being held closed by the weight of fatty tissue. The pair of them were completely immersed in the beast save for a small hole the size of his fist, just big enough to let air in.

And hopefully some of the smell out.

The woman recoiled in horror in the almost pitch darkness, and he felt the tension in her where their bodies touched. He switched on the light on the barrel of his rifle. It lit the interior, where the ribs looked like a vast pink cage enclosing them. But it seemed to help; he felt her slowly ease. She wasn't going to be relaxed, not by a long way, but at least she'd retreated from the edge of hysteria.

"You've got to admit," Wiggo said, "as first dates go, it's got the advantage of originality."

Her laugh was muffled, but he felt her ease even further, and for the first time started to believe they might just get through this.

It's down to the Captain and Wilko now. If they can get to us, we'll be fine. If not..."

He pushed that thought away. Fatalism was for when there were no options, and they weren't there yet.

Yet.

They lay there in silence for a good while. The bear's carcass was slowly cooling around them, but it still retained an amazing amount of heat, like sitting too close to a fire on a cold winter's day. The wind raged and howled outside, but they were almost cozy in their cave.

When Margaret spoke it was with a small, almost childlike voice.

"Talk to me. I'm going stir crazy here."

You and me both, lass.

"Did you have a topic in mind? I've got expertise in blondes, card games and kicking the shit out of big beasties."

"You can tell me about the blondes some other time, and unless you've got a pack of cards handy, that's out too. So beasties it is. You've been taking this all very calmly. I take it you've got a history?"

She settled and he fell backwards slightly against her, so that they were lying like spoons.

"Is that a pistol in your pocket or are you just pleased to see me?" she said.

Any answer to that was going to lead to a conversation best left for another time, so he ignored her and went back to the original topic.

"We're fucking monster magnets, that's what we are," he said, and began at the beginning, with his first op in Antarctica. He tried to give her the abridged versions, and tried to remember not to divulge anything the Colonel in Lossiemouth wouldn't want getting out... which was just about everything if truth be told. But he found some catharsis in it, especially when he got to the ops where young Davies was involved.

"He was just a wee skinny kid from Easterhouse when I first met him," he said softly. "A smart wee bugger, and handy with a gun too. He's had my back these past few years now…or at least, I thought he did."

"He slipped off the path," she said quietly. "It happens."

"Aye. But it's no' supposed to happen to us. Shit, I cannae believe he's gone."

He felt a hand on his shoulder. Suddenly he was fighting back tears.

"Aw fuck," he said quietly. "He was a good lad, and I'm going to miss him. I'm just sorry I was so angry with him near the end there."

"He died saving us."

"Aye, that he did. He was a good soldier."

"And a good man?"

"Aye, that too. One wee slip under duress disnae wipe out all the good, does it?"

"No, it doesn't."

He was all too aware of the heat of her body behind him, but there was nowhere to move away to. She snuggled closer.

He let her.

They had been lying quietly in that manner for a long time. The bear carcass was getting cold faster and Wiggo started to feel the Arctic bite at him.

It'll get me first. She's deeper in, with me to protect her. Even if I'm gone, there'll be a wee bit of extra warmth in it for her. For a while.

The storm had abated somewhat outside; the wind was no longer whistling through the small gap with as much ferocity, and it no longer brought puffs of snow with it. But Wiggo was under no illusions.

We won't last ten minutes outside this bloody thing. And that's erring on the high side. Come on, Cap, where the fuck are you?

The light was starting to dim on his rifle, the battery close to giving up the ghost. He switched it off and put on the one from Davies' weapon. Once that too was gone there'd be nothing but the cold and the dark.

I never thought I'd die lying in the belly of a dead beastie. Then again, I never thought I'd die spooned up against a woman either. Swings and roundabouts, Wiggo, swings and roundabouts.

"Do you hear that?" Margaret said, her lips close to his ear.

"It's just the wind."

"No, listen."

Then he heard it, the faint, but undeniable sound of an engine running.

And it's getting closer.

He struggled his way towards the opening and forced the lips of the wound wide.

"Wait," Margaret said. "What if it's not friendlies?"

"It's transport, lass, and it's what we need. If it's not the Captain and Wilko, I'll take care of it. Trust me, it's what I do best."

"Don't be so sure of that," she said, cryptically, but he had no time to ponder it. The engine noise grew louder still. He clambered out of the belly of the bear. The cold hit him as if he'd run into a wall of ice. His fingers struggled to control his weapon as he unslung it and tried to push his way through a new snowbank around the dead bear.

The engine cut off. Whoever it was, they were just outside the ruins of the dome. The storm had definitely abated; there didn't appear to be any fresh snow making its way inside, and the wind had died off completely. That meant he was able to hear the crunch of footsteps, coming closer.

"If you don't know the fucking password, best not come in," he shouted. "We've got you surrounded."

"You and whose fucking army?" the Captain's well known voice called back, and second later he was face to face with the Captain and Wilkins.

- MARGARET -

She was left to her own devices to get herself out of the carcass. She saw through the gaping wound that the other two soldiers had returned, although they made a strange looking threesome, two of them wearing sealskin suits and Wiggins coated head to toe in gore.

She'd have liked to have made a more dignified entrance to the tableaux for herself, but on exiting the beast her foot caught, again, on the fatty layer and she tumbled out, head first into the snow where she struggled in vain attempts to get to her feet.

Wiggins was by her side and helped her up within seconds. She rose just in time to see the younger officer, Wilkins, grin, and the Captain raise a quizzical eyebrow.

"So you went with the Star Wars defense, Sarge?" Wilkins said. "How was it?"

"Bowfin'," Wiggins replied.

"And Davies? Is he still in there?"

Wilkins made to step forward towards the carcass. Wiggins held him back.

"No, lad. I'm sorry. Davies is up top, somewhere. He saved our lives."

After that there was nothing for it but for them all to return up to the ruined dome and for Wiggins to tell the story while the Captain surveyed the carnage. At least everything was still as they had left it, there had been no further feeding on the bodies, the remains of which were now frozen in place and lightly covered in fresh snow, looking more like the contents of a refrigerated food locker than anything that had once been people. It disguised the horror, but not by much.

Wilkins in particular was taking it sore, and no amount of soft talk from Wiggins was making an impression on his grief. She saw something else in all three of them, something she wasn't even sure they saw themselves. There was steel there, a hardness and resolve she recognised but hadn't seen this close before. These men were family, and they took the Davies lad's death as if they'd lost a brother. It made her slightly guilty at the manner in which she'd been able to file away and compartmentalize the deaths of her own workmates.

"We cannae just leave him like this," Wilkins said, gesturing to where Davies lay.

"No, and we won't," the Captain replied. "But the job comes first."

He turned to Wiggins.

"You say he was trying to get out a message through the Russian's firewall. Did he succeed?"

"I don't know," Wiggins replied. "Everything happened fast. I ken it got sent, but have no idea if it got past them and out into the wild."

"Then we can't wait for a rescue that might never come," Banks replied. He looked down at Davies' body. "I'm about ready to make somebody pay for this. Are you lads with me?"

"Aye," Wilkins said. "Let's finish this."

"All for one and one for all and all that happy shite," Wiggins said. "You know me, Cap, I'm always up for a scrap."

"And you can count me in too," Margaret said, surprising herself. "Just don't make me get inside another of those fucking things. Once is enough for a lifetime."

"Oh, I don't know. I was getting kinda cozy," Wiggins replied.

She cuffed him gently on the ear. Wilkins grinned again, and the Captain did the raised eyebrow thing.

Five minutes later they were out of the dome and beside two large caterpillar-tracked snowmobiles.

"Nice rides," Wiggo said. "I see you've got a story to tell too."

"It'll have to wait. Let's get you inside. The heater's running and the former occupants were kind enough to leave us a flask of coffee. Nae vodka though, more's the pity."

Margaret got in the back of the lead snowmobile. Wiggins got in front with the Captain and a minute later they were driving off, north, away from the dome.

"The Russkis are over there," the Captain said, waving a hand to the west. "Ten miles, maybe a bit more. They'll probably come looking for these vehicles now that the storm has died, so we need to be out of sight, out of mind for a bit. My plan is to circle around and come up behind them. Whether it'll work or not is a toss of the coin, but I don't have much else in the way of resources."

Without any further preamble the Captain filled them in on the part of the story they'd missed, fueled by coffee and smokes passed back and forth in the cramped cabin. They kept driving north, the headlights picking out nothing but snow-covered ground. Margaret knew there were crevasses and weak points out here on the ice, but figured that was the least of her worries at that moment. She tried to keep her attention on the Captain's story, but, despite the coffee and smokes, tiredness was washing over her in waves. She forced herself to pay attention, until the Captain's part was done.

"Why us?" she said when the man was obviously finished.

"'Live animal testing,' that's what the man said," Banks replied. "I guess they figured they could get away with almost anything that they wanted to do out here in the middle of nowhere."

"Fucking cowboys," Wiggins muttered.

"Cossacks, more like," Banks replied. "But whoever they are, they're not going to be here much longer."

There was that steel again, and a glint in the man's eyes. She resolved never to get on this team's bad side…it wasn't likely to end well for her.

There didn't seem to be any prospect of the Captain slowing anytime soon. Indeed, he might have already started that slow turn he'd mentioned earlier. There was no way for Margaret to know. All she could see was the backs of the two men's heads and the bleak prospect of more ice and snow-covered ground in front of them. The purr and throb of the engine served only to lull her into ever deeper tiredness. Wiggins said something to her but she didn't catch it and as quickly as turning out a light, she fell asleep for the first time in three days.

- WILKINS-

Wilkins tried to concentrate on just following the snowmobile ahead of him, but his mind kept spinning round on him, showing him lurid photos of Davies' mutilated body lying frozen in the snow. He imagined Davies looking up at him, a sullen look in his eyes.

Are you happy now?

Those hadn't been the last words spoken between them.

But they might as well have been.

There would be no reconciliation over a beer or curry, no more sharing banter about their respective sex lives, or lack of same. They'd come into the squad together on the same op, but now Wilkins was going to have to go on alone. He'd used up much of his mental fortitude just to come back from his leg injuries.

I'm going to need a lot more for this.

He pushed the thoughts away again, trying to compartmentalize them where he could take them out and pursue them dispassionately at a later date. As the captain had said, the job comes first.

I just wish I could make myself believe it.

Up front the captain was forcing the snowmobile along at a good clip. The storm had cleared off, and a blanket of stars was being drawn on the sky as the clouds dissipated. Normally Wilkins would be looking up in awe, drinking in the majesty of it. But not today. His legs ached, but not as much as his heart. He looked in the rear view mirror, peering into the gloom behind them, but there was no sign of the ruined domes, just darkness.

Darkness, and Davies lying in it, alone.

He pushed that thought away too. A glance at the compass told him that the Captain had started making a slow turn to the west. There would be action ahead.

He was looking forward to it.

Wilkins almost leapt out of his seat when a speaker in front of the steering column blared into life.

"Hey, is this fucker on?"

"Sarge?"

"Well, it ain't no sanity clause," Wiggo replied in an atrocious mock Italian accent that Wilkins couldn't help but laugh at.

"You okay back there, wee man?" Wiggo continued.

"Warm but not exactly cozy, Sarge. I'm ready for some payback."

"And so say all of us. That's why I'm on the line. The Cap says he can see the light of the complex in the distance. Follow his lead, and watch out in case we have to make a sudden stop. And keep your eyes peeled for bears. We don't ken how many of those fuckers might be roaming around out here."

Now that the Sarge had mentioned it, Wilkins was able to spot the distinctive blue glow in the sky ahead that marked the existence of the compound on the ground. His compass told him they'd come all the way around it and were now approaching it from the far side from where they'd been earlier. The Captain's plan was working, so far.

But we're just getting to the tricky bit.

The Captain brought his snowmobile to a halt at least half a mile away from the Russian complex and dimmed his lights. Wilkins pulled up behind him and followed suit. The speaker burst into life again.

"Have a smoke and a rest, lad," Wiggo said. "The Cap and I are going for a reccy."

"What about the woman?"

"She's having a kip in the back. Just leave her be. She's been through the wringer."

There was just enough light for him to make out the bulk of the snowmobile in front of him. He caught a hint of two darker shadows moving away, then all fell quiet.

He took Wiggo's advice and lit up a smoke, but now that he was still again, the thoughts and recriminations began to crowd in around him.

I should have known something was wrong with him. The signs were there in Orkney.

But back then Wilkins was still in recovery, still coming to terms with injuries of his own. His had been to the body, but Davies' had been deeper, tearing at his spirit until the only way he could see out was through the morphine.

What must he have gone through, holding all that pain in?

It was a question Wilkins couldn't answer, one he'd never get an answer to now.

He really hoped the Captain's plan involved some swift action.

I've got a friend to avenge.

He'd been wool-gathering for several minutes when the door at his passenger side swung open with a crash and once again he nearly leapt up in the air. His hand instinctively went for his weapon, and it was only at the last instant he pulled the barrel aside. It was the woman, Margaret.

"For pity's sake, don't do that. I near pished myself," he said as she climbed up into the seat.

"Sorry. I woke up in the dark and..."

She didn't have to say anything. It was dim in the snowmobile cockpit, only the dashboard lights for illumination, but he saw that the Sarge hadn't been wrong. In fact she looked like she'd been through a wringer both literally and metaphorically. Wilkins had seen people on the edge before. She looked ready to tip over it.

"You got any smokes?" she said. "Your sergeant's buggered off with all we had."

Wilkins took out the pack he'd 'liberated' from one of the guards at the Russian compound.

"These are a bit rough," he said.

"Hah. My old granddad used to let me have a puff of his Capstan Full Strength. Can't be any rougher than that."

I wouldn't bet on it.

But despite the warning, she took to the cigarette eagerly enough, sucking in smoke and not letting much of it back out. She saw him looking.

"I'll worry about my lungs tomorrow."

If Wiggo had been here, there would have followed a quip about her lungs looking just fine. Indeed, she looked like she was half-expecting it from him.

Wilkins laughed.

"I don't do flirting," he said. "At least not like the Sarge. My predilections lie elsewhere."

She reddened as she realized what he'd implied.

"Sorry," she said.

"I'm not. But you've obviously been around the Sarge long enough now to know what to expect."

"He's a good man," she said. "Better than he gives himself credit for."

"We all know that."

"He's badly cut up about the dead lad. He blames himself."

"Well, I blame myself too. And sure the Cap's also thought it. It's who we are."

She was looking out the window into the darkness.

"The boy died hard. They all did."

"And if there's anyone to blame, it's the folk in that compound down there," he answered. "Don't go taking onto yourself what isn't yours to carry."

"Now you sound like Wiggins."

"He must be rubbing off on me too."

"Chance would be a fine thing," Margaret said, and suddenly, just like that they were both roaring with laughter.

They were still laughing a minute later when the Captain and Wiggo returned.

- WIGGO-

The Captain had told Wiggo about the scale of the Russian operation, but he hadn't been able to wrap his head around it until he'd seen it for himself. Now, back in the snowmobile, all four of them crowded into the one vehicle, he had questions.

"How are we going to take it down, Cap? There's only the three of us and they outnumber us ten to one by the look of it. And that's before we take into account the fucking enormous bears."

"Four of us," Margaret said quietly. "There's four of us."

"Aye. But when the fighting starts, you're staying here," Wiggo answered.

"Don't I get a say?"

"Nope."

"We'll see about that," she replied, then fell quiet when the Captain spoke.

"I'm working on it," he said. "But I don't think you're going to like it."

"Hah," Wilkins added. "The last time you said that I found myself standing alone in front of a charging bear. I'm not falling for that line again."

"If there's any volunteering to be done this time, I'm calling first dibs," Wiggo interrupted. "And I'm not taking any questions."

"No, I need you here with the vehicles," Banks said. "Wilkins and I will be taking a wee walk to retrieve the snowmobiles and then it'll be showtime."

"What have you got in mind, Cap?" Wiggo asked.

"I'm thinking it's time we got the temperature up all over the camp."

"Ah, I do like the old stories."

The Captain laid out his plan, they synchronized their watches, and Wilkins and the Cap left for their walk around the perimeter.

"It's not much of a plan," Margaret said. She and Wiggo were sitting up front in the lead snowmobile. His orders were to not move until five o' clock, and then head for the Russian installation and wait for a signal. They were sharing a cigarette.

"To be fair to the Captain, we don't have much by way of resources."

"Just promise you'll be back," she said. "I don't mind minding the snowmobile. What I would mind would be being left alone with it for eternity."

"I'll be back, lass, that's a promise," Wiggo said, and meant it. He'd left enough behind on this op already, he wasn't about to lose anybody more. He checked his watch.

"Time I got moving," he said. "Are you sure you don't want a handgun?"

They'd already been over this; Wiggo wanted her to take a weapon, she refused point blank.

"I'm more likely to shoot my tits off than hit anything," she said.

"Aye, well, we cannae have that, can we. You might have some use for them when this show's over."

Her smile was the last he saw of her as he got out of the snowmobile.

"I might at that," she said, then shut the door on him before he could ruin the moment.

The second snowmobile was only five yards ahead, but no more than a dark shadow as its lights were off and Wiggo had orders to keep it that way. He climbed inside, made sure his rifle wasn't going to be impeded if he had to get to it fast, and started up the engine in low revs.

"You'll have to be sneaky," the Cap had said.

"I'm not sure I ken how," Wiggo had replied, but he knew his job well enough… the Cap had been explicit.

"Creep up to the ridge above the complex, don't get caught, and wait for my signal."

Even I can't fuck this one up.

There was enough diffuse blue light ahead for him to get a bead on his destination. Staying in low revs he crept forward slowly, no lights showing. There was no rush, he had a good ten minutes before showtime. He lit a cigarette and allowed himself a small prayer that the woman would be okay on her own, then turned his mind to the job at hand.

He arrived at the lip of the sunken hollow above the Russian complex with ninety seconds to spare; any longer and there'd be too big a risk of being spotted, any later and he might miss the signal. He counted down the time on his watch.

With thirty seconds to go he stepped outside, located the fuel line and cut it.

With twenty seconds to go he revved up the engine to full throttle.

Ten seconds to go he put the machine in drive and it trundled closer to the lip.

Dead on time there was an explosion on the far side of the hollow. A burning Skidoo came over the lip and bulleted down the hill towards the great tent, trailing flame all the way.

Wiggo kept the driver's door open as he rolled the big snowmobile up to the lip. It teetered on the edge, then hit the slope. For a bad second he thought it was going to topple, taking him with it, but it straightened. He had it aimed straight at the tent. Once he was sure of its trajectory he flicked on his Zippo lighter.

"I'm going to miss you," he said to the lighter.

He threw himself out the open door and in the same movement tossed the burning lighter into the trail of fuel just behind the snowmobile. The vehicle was picking up speed now, its engine roaring. A snake of fire followed it down the hill.

Wiggo followed it down, sliding on his backside and hoping he didn't hit any big bumps along the way. He saw the Skidoo reach bottom on the far side of the complex, reach the tent and immediately start a fire.

Klaxons sounded almost immediately, but they were too late to stop the inevitable. While the Russians' attention was on the smaller fire, the big snowmobile lumbered, nowhere near as graceful as a bear but just as effective, into the tent, getting caught in the folds of material. There was a whump, and an explosion that lit up the whole complex.

The tent went up like a sheet of paper dropped in a fireplace just as Wiggo reached the bottom of the hill. He swung his rifle off his shoulder and made for the sounds of screaming.

This is for Davies.

- WILKINS-

Wilkins sat in the rear seat of the second Skidoo behind the Captain, watching as the flaming Skidoo barreled down the slope and into the tent. He held his breath when he saw Wiggo's snowmobile trailing flame on the far side of the hollow, and almost let out a cheer when it set the structure aflame in a conflagration.

"My cunning plan is working. Hang on, lad," Banks shouted, and set the Skidoo over the lip. They went down the hill in a blur of speed as exhilarating as any toboggan ride. There were several moments Wilkins was sure they were going to topple over and see themselves crushed beneath the bike, but the Captain rode the bucks and throws with seemingly expert ease. They hit the bottom of the slope, still accelerating.

The Captain showed no sign of slowing. The area where the Skidoo had hit was well ablaze. There was a flurry of activity around the fire as workers and soldiers tried to organize a response. The Captain wasn't about to give them any time for that; he aimed the bike directly at the fire and gunned it to full throttle, at the same time unslinging his rifle. Wilkins followed suit.

As they neared the tent two of the Russian soldiers finally took note of them. They reached for their weapons; that was as far as they got. The Captain took out the one on the left, Wilkins the one on the right and the Skidoo was past them before their bodies hit the ground.

The tent was well aflame where the Skidoo had run into it, but the bigger fire by far was on the far side of the complex. The sky over in that direction flared in reds and oranges and thick black smoke rose to obscure the stars. The air was filled with sound, even above the clatter of the Skidoo. Klaxons blared, sirens wailed, people, some of them on fire, screamed and, from somewhere inside the tent, great bears roared, frenzied to be free.

And still the Captain showed no sign of stopping. He headed straight for an opening in the tent that was ringed in flame.

- MARGARET-

She didn't hear the explosion, but she saw the red glare grow in the sky some way ahead of her position. She hoped it was a sign that the Captain's plan was working. She considered stepping outside the snowmobile to see if she could hear anything, but thought better of it; Wiggins' instructions had been short, and to the point.

"Don't you fucking dare go outside. And no moving from this spot. If any Russians come along, play dumb until we come to get you."

Dumb I can do.

She was trying to content herself with watching the light show when the dashboard in front of her lit up and one of the screens started to beep at her.

What now?

She knew nothing about the array of instruments in front of her.

But I know enough to spot a tracking system when I see one.

The circular blue screen showed a red dot at the outer rim. The dot was moving, heading inwards.

Whatever it is, it's coming this way. That can't be good.

She dropped her gaze from the red glow and tried to scan the horizon, but it was too dark to see much of anything.

The red dot was still coming closer.

The speaker system in the snowmobile burst into life and an excited, somewhat scared, voice shouted something in Russian that she had no way to respond to. In the background she heard gunfire. Once again, she could only hope the Captain's plan was working.

She was still holding on to that hope when a white bear lumbered out of the darkness, right in front of the snowmobile. Even though she was sitting high in the cockpit, its head was level with hers. It stood perfectly still, staring in at her as if searching her soul.

She remembered the Captain's words about the little black box.

The bloody thing is waiting for instructions.

She had no way of giving it any, short of pushing every button and twisting every dial on the dashboard, and didn't think much of that plan.

So they sat there, in the cold dark, just watching each other.

Margaret wondered who would be first to twitch.

- WIGGO-

Wiggo's orders had been simple enough.

Find the comms trailer and fuck it up.

It had sounded simple in theory, but the theory hadn't mentioned a fucking huge fire, scores of angry, screaming Russians, some with guns, blinding smoke…oh, and some very angry giant-sized polar bears who were now out of their cages, and, if not quite out of control, at least not very happy.

Wiggo swerved and dashed in and out between the trailers. He remembered the Captain telling him that the comms trailer was near the main entrance; that meant it was on the other side of the tent from where he'd started. He was currently somewhere halfway around the perimeter, and the chaos around him was seriously slowing his progress.

At least nobody's noticed me yet.

As he got closer to the main entrance he saw that the Captain and Wilkins had also been busy. The tent was also aflame here, but it was more under control. He saw soldiers carrying bodies away, and had a bad moment when he thought they might be his companions. Then he heard gunfire from inside the tent, and the distinctive rattle and clack of a snowmobile.

Go get them, lads.

Finally he caught a glimpse of a trailer ahead that was festooned in aerials and small satellite dishes.

Bingo!

He made for it at a run.

Finally somebody took notice of him, he heard a yell... 'stop' sounds the same in just about any language, but Wiggo wasn't going to pay it any heed in any case. A soldier stepped in front of him, just starting to raise a rifle. Wiggo went through him like a dose of salts, a three-shot burst almost blowing the man's head off. More shouts rose up, and a shot zinged past Wiggo's head, pinging off the trailer. Wiggo didn't bother to look. He raised his weapon and sent round after round into the array of aerials and dishes, blowing them into scattered fragments of plastic and metal.

Another bullet tugged at the hood of his parka.

He spun round, spraying shots in a defensive arc even as he tumbled and rolled to a kneeling position, taking aim in the same movement. There were two of them and it was like shooting ducks in a barrel. They were down and dead before they knew it.

There were more sounds of gunfire, from inside the tent again. Wiggo had completed his orders, as far as they'd been given. Now it was time to join the others.

He headed towards the tent. The fire was out here now but he could see that the far end was totally ablaze, a conflagration reaching high into the sky, and pieces of burning canvas were falling to drape over the trailers in that direction. They were going to reach the central dome soon.

There was no sign of the Captain or young Wilkins, and Wiggo was about to go in search of them when a roar from his left caught his attention.

He turned in time to see one of the great bears smash its way out of a cage. It was no longer controlled, no longer docile, and it did not look happy in the slightest.

There were cages all around the perimeter of the tent, and bears were smashing against the bars in all of them. It was only going to be a matter of time before they all escaped.

Then the real fun's going to start.

- WILKINS-

They met with little resistance as they made their way into the complex's central dome. The far end of the tent was well ablaze and every able bodied man in the area was over in that direction attempting to get the fire under control. It looked like it was going to be a losing battle.

"This whole bloody thing is going to go up," Wilkins said.

"I fucking well hope so," Banks replied. "And it'll take us with it if we don't hurry."

"What are we after?"

"Just the one thing."

Banks brought the Skidoo to a halt outside the dome entrance. Again, they met no one as they made their way inside. A klaxon bleated incessantly and the air, even inside the dome, was rapidly filling with smoke.

The Russian commander was sitting behind his desk smoking one of his foul cigarettes and nursing a large glass of vodka. There was a pistol on the table in front of him.

"Do you know what you've done?" the Russian said.

"Aye, and I know what I'm about to do next," Banks said. "You're coming with me. My bosses will have questions."

"As will mine," the Russian said. "Unfortunately, I have decided to answer neither."

He went for the gun.

Wilkins and Banks had both anticipated the move and were raising their weapons, but they were too late. The Russian jammed the barrel under his chin, pulled the trigger and blew most of his brains out onto the wall behind him.

"At least we won't have to lug him around with us," Wilkins said.

"Aye, a small mercy."

The smoke was getting thicker, the klaxon more insistent, and they saw an orange glow overhead in the opaque dome; the fire was almost overhead.

"Time we were leaving," Banks said, and the pair of them left the dome at a run.

Pieces of burning canvas fell all around them and the whole far end of the tent sagged inwards alarmingly.

They got the Skidoo going in time to avoid one of the larger fragments coming down on top of them and headed back out into the main tent just as the burning canvas fell over the dome and started to consume it.

The Captain aimed the Skidoo directly for the main entrance. As they approached it they saw that the bears were loose, and gathering around the way out of the tent. They were also showing an interest in Wiggo. The sergeant was slowly backing away from three of them who stalked him like big cats after a meal.

"Wiggo, to me," the Captain shouted and skidded the Skidoo to a halt just feet from the sergeant. Wiggo retreated towards them. At the same moment the bears, not just the three nearest ones but the others, at least two dozen in the doorway, all raised their heads and sniffed at the air. A collective roar rang out from all of them, and their gaze fell on Wilkins and the captain.

They've got the scent of the sealskin clothes.

"I guess we know what's for lunch," Banks said. "Climb on anywhere you can manage, Sarge. And hold on. I'm not going to be hanging about."

Wiggo climbed aboard, crushing Wilkins in a sandwich between him and the Captain up front.

The Captain gunned the Skidoo, just in time. He aimed it back into the tent away from the gathered bears and hit the throttle. With the three of them aboard the Skidoo complained and dragged but at least they were on the move.

The beasts broke into a loping run chasing after them.

- MARGARET -

The red glow in the sky behind the bear grew steadily more intense but the bear hadn't taken any note of it. It continued to stand there staring almost vacantly at the snowmobile.

Then it shivered all over, as if it had taken a shock, and when it looked up again it had much more life in its eyes and much less docility. It took a step towards the snowmobile.

Margaret was at a loss as to what to do, so did the only thing she could think of; she switched on the big front headlights. The bear reacted instantly, standing up on its hind legs, looming over the vehicle, its roaring bellow easily heard through the reinforced windows. It came back down on its front paws with a thud that sent snow and ice flying, and launched itself forward.

It hit the snowmobile like an oncoming train, pushing the vehicle backwards even as its great paws threw a blow at the window. The window held, but Margaret was being shaken around like a sock in a clothes dryer. She squirmed into the driver's seat and turned on the engine, putting her foot down hard on the accelerator pedal.

The bear barely shifted at first, all its attention was on trying to get at Margaret through the glass, but as the caterpillar tracks started to get traction she began to push the beast backwards. She had hoped that it would just give up against the obvious strength of the vehicle, but it kept pushing against the weight and Margaret had to keep her foot all the way down on the pedal.

The snowmobile squealed in complaint.

Margaret hit the horn.

The bear roared back at it

Margaret knew they were heading towards the Russian complex, slowly but surely making for the lip of the ridge that dropped off into the hollow. She had no idea what she was going to do when they reached it, but she couldn't afford to take her foot off the pedal and give the bear another chance to attack the window.

They inched forward at little more than walking speed, heading for the drop off that Margaret knew was there but couldn't see past the body of the beast.

She put her foot down as hard as she could, hit the horn continually... and prayed for a miracle.

- WIGGO-

Wiggo turned to watch the chase. The leader of the pack of bears was only ten yards behind the Skidoo, and closing. Wiggo reached round to unsling his rifle, and in the process nearly overbalanced the bike.

"For fuck's sake, Sarge," Banks shouted from the front, "I'm having enough trouble with this thing as it is without you dancing about in the back."

Wiggo didn't reply, he was too busy taking aim. He knew head shots hardly slowed these beasts down, so he tried another tack; he shot out the front bear's left knee and it went down in a tumble of arms and legs. Two of the other bears gave up the chase and started tearing at it in a frenzy. The area around it turned red with gore in seconds.

"One down," he shouted.

"Aye, and twenty to go," Banks replied. "Give me a second, I've got a plan."

And we're not going to like it.

The Captain slowly turned the Skidoo so that they were racing headlong towards where the great tent was most aflame. Most of the material was burning now, huge sails of it drooping towards the compound floor. It looked like most of the Russian staff had been caught in the conflagration, and those that hadn't were being mopped up by ravaging bears.

Ahead of them, a massive flap of cloth, a sheet of fire, was slowly dropping towards the floor. Beyond that they could see the darkness of the outside world, but the gap was closing fast.

"We're not going to make it," Wiggo shouted.

The bears were right on their heels now, a snarling wall of white rage. Wiggo put down another one by shooting its legs out from under it, but this time none of the others stopped; they had the scent of a squaddie and knew what they wanted.

The Skidoo sped towards the ever narrowing gap. The burning cloth was overhead now and it was as if they'd driven head first into a raging hot oven. Wiggo was finding it hard to breathe. Black smoke obscured his vision. There was nothing but the clatter of the Skidoo, the roar of bears and the ever growing threat of being burned under the falling tent.

Then he saw the gap, only forty yards ahead but closing fast. The falling cloth was only feet overhead, dripping fire all around them. He brushed ash from Wilkins' parka that had been smoldering there, threatening to set it alight. The Skidoo, at full throttle, rattled and whined. Steam was coming from the engine and it sounded wheezy and hoarse.

If it dies on us now, we're toast.

They reached the gap with no more than a foot of air to spare overhead and burst out into immediate relief in the cold. The Captain skidded the Skidoo to a stop and they all wheeled round, weapons raised, waiting for the bears.

No attack came. The tent collapsed completely and all that could be seen of the animals was writhing, burning shapes under the fallen canopy. The roars of pain were terrible enough in themselves, but the accompanying smell of burning flesh made Wiggo want to retch.

They stood there for several minutes while the tent finally consumed everything underneath it.

No bears made it out.

No Russians either.

Wiggo realized he'd been hearing something for several seconds without it registering. He turned towards the source of the sound just in time to see the snowmobile arrive at the ridge. It looked like it was in a wrestling match with one of the bears. The animal was threatening to lose its balance right on the edge of the hollow.

And if it does, it'll bring the lassie down with it.

Wiggo didn't stop to think. He swung his weapon round, took aim and squeezed off three shots.

The bear's back legs gave out under it and it toppled away towards them down the slope. The snowmobile teetered for a second on the edge, then rocked backwards and stayed in place.

- MARGARET -

The next few hours passed in a blur for Margaret.

She had still been processing the fact that she was still alive when the three squad members returned on a battered Skidoo. The Captain took charge again, taking the snowmobile back towards the Research Station. They had one last look down at the still burning remnants of the Russian complex before they left.

"That's some real James Bond shit right there," Margaret said and Wiggo, who was in the back seats beside her, laughed.

"The villain's dastardly scheme is thwarted, his secret base is destroyed…and our hero gets the girl."

"Not so fast, chummy," she replied. "I'll need a smoke first."

They hadn't been back at the Research Station site for more than an hour when the rescue flight arrived. She'd been herded aboard, and immediately looked around for the squad members to see if they were coming up behind her.

"They're staying behind to help with the clear up," she'd been told.

And that was the last she'd seen of them until a week later when an invitation to a funeral came in the post. She'd already attended a memorial service for the Research Station dead and didn't think she could handle any more, but when she turned the card over there was a personal message for her.

"Please come. I'd like to see you."

Two days later she was standing in a wet and miserable graveyard in the East Side of Glasgow. The squad members were there, along with Davies' mother, two black youths and a man who introduced himself as Sergeant Hynd. He had the same steel in him as the members of the squad.

A piper played a lament, a minister gave a brief eulogy that said almost nothing about the dead man, and then it was done. She was about to turn away when Wiggo came up to her.

He took her by the hand.

"The Sarge, my auld Sarge that is, suggested we go for dinner. His wife's coming along. Would you, that is…"

For once, it seemed, Wiggo was lost for words.

"I thought you'd never ask," she said and, taking his arm, they walked off after the others.

CHECK OUT OTHER GREAT CRYPTID NOVELS

BIGFOOT WAR
by **Eric S. Brown**

Now a feature film from Origin Releasing. For the first time ever, all three core books of the Bigfoot War series have been collected into a single tome of Sasquatch Apocalypse horror. Remastered and reedited this book chronicles the original war between man and beast from the initial battles in Babblecreek through the apocalypse to the wastelands of a dark future world where Sasquatch reigns supreme and mankind struggles to survive. If you think you've experienced Bigfoot Horror before, think again. Bigfoot War sets the bar for the genre and will leave you praying that you never have to go into the woods again.

CRYPTID ZOO
by **Gerry Griffiths**

As a child, rare and unusual animals, especially cryptid creatures, always fascinated Carter Wilde.

Now that he's an eccentric billionaire and runs the largest conglomerate of high-tech companies all over the world, he can finally achieve his wildest dream of building the most incredible theme park ever conceived on the planet...CRYPTID ZOO.

Even though there have been apparent problems with the project, Wilde still decides to send some of his marketing employees and their families on a forced vacation to assess the theme park in preparation for Opening Day.

Nick Wells and his family are some of those chosen and are about to embark on what will become the most terror-filled weekend of their lives—praying they survive.

STEP RIGHT UP AND GET YOUR FREE PASS...

TO CRYPTID ZOO

CHECK OUT OTHER GREAT CRYPTID NOVELS

SWAMP MONSTER MASSACRE
by **Hunter Shea**

The swamp belongs to them. Humans are only prey. Deep in the overgrown swamps of Florida, where humans rarely dare to enter, lives a race of creatures long thought to be only the stuff of legend. They walk upright but are stronger, taller and more brutal than any man. And when a small boat of tourists, held captive by a fleeing criminal, accidentally kills one of the swamp dwellers' young, the creatures are filled with a terrifyingly human emotion—a merciless lust for vengeance that will paint the trees red with blood.

TERROR MOUNTAIN
by **Gerry Griffiths**

When Marcus Pike inherits his grandfather's farm and moves his family out to the country, he has no idea there's an unholy terror running rampant about the mountainous farming community. Sheriff Avery Anderson has seen the heinous carnage and the mutilated bodies. He's also seen the giant footprints left in the snow—Bigfoot tracks. Meanwhile, Cole Wagner, and his wife, Kate, are prospecting their gold claim farther up the valley, unaware of the impending dangers lurking in the woods as an early winter storm sets in. Soon the snowy countryside will run red with blood on TERROR MOUNTAIN.

CHECK OUT OTHER GREAT CRYPTID NOVELS

RETURN TO DYATLOV PASS
by J.H. Moncrieff

In 1959, nine Russian students set off on a skiing expedition in the Ural Mountains. Their mutilated bodies were discovered weeks later. Their bizarre and unexplained deaths are one of the most enduring true mysteries of our time. Nearly sixty years later, podcast host Nat McPherson ventures into the same mountains with her team, determined to finally solve the mystery of the Dyatlov Pass incident. Her plans are thwarted on the first night, when two trackers from her group are brutally slaughtered. The team's guide, a superstitious man from a neighboring village, blames the killings on yetis, but no one believes him. As members of Nat's team die one by one, she must figure out if there's a murderer in their midst—or something even worse—before history repeats itself and her group becomes another casualty of the infamous Dead Mountain.

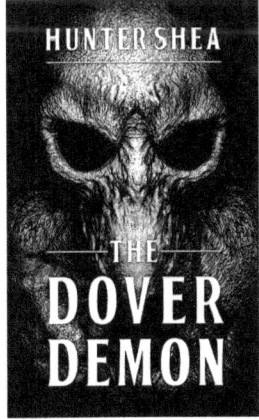

DOVER DEMON
by Hunter Shea

The Dover Demon is real...and it has returned. In 1977, Sam Brogna and his friends came upon a terrifying, alien creature on a deserted country road. What they witnessed was so bizarre, so chilling, they swore their silence. But their lives were changed forever. Decades later, the town of Dover has been hit by a massive blizzard. Sam's son, Nicky, is drawn to search for the infamous cryptid, only to disappear into the bowels of a secret underground lair. The Dover Demon is far deadlier than anyone could have believed. And there are many of them. Can Sam and his reunited friends rescue Nicky and battle a race of creatures so powerful, so sinister, that history itself has been shaped by their secretive presence?